The Help of a Cowboy

Crossroads Creek Cowboys

Elsie Davis

Sweet Romance Publishing

@2022 Elsie Davis

All rights reserved. Except as permitted under the U.S. Copyright Act of 1976, no part of this publication may be reproduced, distributed or transmitted in any form or by any means, or stored in a database or retrieval system without the prior written permission of the publisher.

Cover Design by getcovers.com

Edited by Elaine Hyatt (Clarity Editing Services) & Cassandra Cornell

This is a work of fiction. Names, characters, organizations, places, events, and incidents are either products of the author's imagination or are used fictitiously. Any resemblance to actual persons, living or dead, or actual events is purely coincidental.

Sweet Romance Publishing

Sweetromancepublishing.com

PO Box 778

Liberty, NC 27298

Luke 6:37

"Do not judge, and you will not be judged.

Do not condemn, and you will not be con-
demned.

Forgive, and you will be forgiven."

Chapter One

♥

"Lady, you're trespassing," Chad said, gently reining in Duchess. His mare stopped short several feet from a woman and a young girl, possibly her daughter judging by the similar coloring of their fair skin and golden blonde hair. Strangely enough, the two appeared to be setting up for a picnic, and of all things—*on his land*.

The woman spun around, her mouth forming a wide "O". She grasped the child's hand, pulling her close as if to protect the little girl from the big, bad wolf.

Only neither one looked like Little Red Riding Hood, and this wasn't a fairytale. "You're trespassing," he repeated, eager to have them gone and be on his way. Chad didn't have time for socialization with travelers passing through the area who had a misguided notion of right and wrong.

"I'm s-sorry. The rail was down and it's such a pretty spot, with all the flowers in bloom, so I thought to check it out, maybe take some pictures. We meant no harm, I promise," the woman talked fast, sounding like a northeast-erner. She pushed a few strands of long hair back from her face and gazed up at him with blue eyes the color of the deep sea.

Chad frowned. "You thought wrong. Not sure where you come from, but this is Crossroads Creek. Around here, a fence means private property." Duchess shook her head as if in agreement, but more than likely it was a move to keep the flies away.

"The south doesn't have a lock on the meaning, as it's the same in New York City. Mostly. In my defense, this property is for sale. Therefore, the assumption is the place is open to viewing. And by the looks of things," she glanced at the downed split rail, and then gestured to the open fields, "I figured no one was living here anymore."

The woman was getting on his nerves with her fast-talking city explanation. "Again, another incorrect assumption. It's past time you were leaving," he added, cutting to the crux of the situation. The farm took up every minute of his life, something he planned to change when the place finally sold, but until then, he was losing daylight.

"You don't have to be so rude about it. The Texas Bluebonnets were incredible in all their glory in this field and I found them hard to resist. I only wanted twenty minutes to stretch and have a bite to eat, not steal your boss's cattle...even though it doesn't look like he has any." She huffed, glancing around as if to make her point.

His boss? That was a joke. And as of last week, Chad was the only one left working on the farm. Money was tight, and he'd been pairing down, scrimping to hold it all together. "You're lucky I came along then. You would have less than five minutes before the bull in yonder pasture," he flicked his head to the right, "got wind of food and came to investigate."

The woman inhaled sharply, grabbed up the blanket and backpack, and took a step closer to the fence. "Bull?" She glanced around, her eyes darting back and forth across the area.

Miss High and Mighty suddenly seemed out of sorts. "Bull. As in a big, two-thousand-pound, in-your-face animal. A Holstein, to be exact." It was a stretch, but the woman didn't know it. The bull part was true, but Ruffian was in another pasture with much better fencing to keep him locked up and away from what herd he had left. People didn't understand that fences weren't always just to keep people out, sometimes it was to keep them safe from the animals inside the area.

"We'll leave," she said, lifting her daughter up and over the mid-level rail to safety as if she couldn't get out of there fast enough.

"Glad to hear it. If you think the place is so beautiful, you could always buy it," he added, never one to miss an opportunity to find a buyer and unload the albatross, holding him back from what he really wanted—a life in the city. *One that didn't come with all the responsibilities of a dairy farm.*

The woman's chin rose a notch. "Well, maybe I'll just do that." After climbing over the rail herself, she led her daughter toward the car parked by the road.

Judging by the over-packed old Buick with its sun-faded blue paint, the woman didn't have enough money to buy his barn, much less the entire farm. "You and what miracle?" he taunted, amused by her efforts to stay on the winning end of the conversation, when she had clearly been in the wrong.

Blue eyes shot him an icy glare. "I'll have you know—"

"Mommy, I've got to go to the bathroom," the young girl said, reminding him of his little sister when she was that age.

Experience told him the mother needed to listen or there would be consequences. Chad had learned the hard way. But it only took once. It was a long time ago, back when it was just the two of them against a mean world. A time well before Roxanne had grown up, met Hank, and fell in love. Most assuredly, those days were long gone. Just like his sister was long gone from the farm now that she was married and had moved into town. It was the event in his life that finally prompted the for-sale sign to go up.

"Okay, Lindsey. Get in the car and put on your seatbelt. I'm sure there's a place in Crossroads Creek where we can stop." She pulled open the back door and helped her daughter up into her booster seat.

"Place called Courtney's Deli is new in town...good sandwiches since it looks like you'll be missing your picnic. Or you could try the Golden Spoon diner. Beverly Jenkins owns the place and has been in business since I can remember. She's not uptight cranky like some places that don't want non-paying customers using the restrooms," Chad offered. The woman was leaving and he could afford to be nice now that they were on the same page.

Unlike old man Beasley, who hadn't been so kind to Roxanne, the result was more than enough humiliation for his sister when she peed her pants. The man was dead and gone now, but the attitudes of people in town hadn't changed much toward him. They still hated Chad's father, and by extension, Chad himself. The town totally believed the sins of the father should be visited upon the children and nothing had changed in ten years. Not that Chad gave them much of a chance to lord it over him. He avoided the town like the plague, preferring to do business elsewhere for his own peace of mind.

"Thanks, I will." The woman shot him a smile that softened his heart.

Breathtaking was the word that came to mind. Not a word he used often, if ever. A moment of weakness in response to the overture of kindness. Apparently, his early rudeness had been forgiven with his small offer of help. Chad tipped his hat, watched her climb in the car, and drive away.

"What do you think, Duchess? Any chance she was serious about buying the place? We don't get many strangers around here." Duchess snorted. Chad leaned forward to pat the side of her neck. "Sorry, girl. I know you don't like me to talk about selling the place. I promise I'll make sure you have an amazing new owner. It's the least I could do for you. I'd take you with me if horses were allowed inside a Dallas apartment. Somehow, I don't think you'd fit...or like it much, for that matter." Chad chuckled. Leaving Duchess behind was one of the few things that bothered him with his decision. The two had been a pair for nigh on fifteen years, and with that, was an unbreakable bond. Apart, but together in heart forever.

Chad pulled out his phone, the woman's words sinking in. On the off chance the woman made an offer on the place, his realtor might hold hard on the selling price. If there was ever a time to be proactive, this might be it. Chad called his friend, not having to wait long before Paul answered. "I need to go over something with you."

"Well, hello to you, too. I know you want to sell the ranch, but it's a buyer's market right now. That might change in a year or so, but I've already explained all this to you," Paul said, assuming about the reason for the call.

"You did, and it's why I'm calling you. I don't want to wait another year and I'm not sure I can keep the place running that long on the bare-bones budget I've got set aside to last me. I really thought some rich cowboy wannabe would scoop the place up," Chad said, urging Duchess forward.

"You never know. It's a small ranch by most people's standards."

"Three-hundred acres isn't that small." Chad frowned. Once upon a time he might have expanded, but no one in town would sell their land to him, even if he had tried. The folks in town were good people, but their memory was sharper than a tack. Not even ten years had dulled their memory of when Jim Thompson robbed the town bank at gunpoint, accidentally killing the sheriff. His father was the most notorious name in Crossroads Creek.

Oddly enough, he was a little surprised someone from town hadn't bought the place already, if only to see Chad leave town. He wasn't sure how his sister tolerated the folks in town, but he'd found limited socialization to be a great cure.

"So what's up?" Paul asked.

"I just caught some woman and her kid trespassing. She just left but made a comment about buying the place. Just in case she stops by to see you, I would like for you to be more than accommodating." Her response had been to his own taunt, but still, maybe it was enough to plant the seed.

"Accommodating how, just to be clear? And what's her name?" Paul asked.

Chad frowned. "I don't know her story, or the first thing about her, including her name. We met under unusual circumstances, and it wasn't on the friendliest of terms. I reckon her husband plans on joining her soon. But if she wants to buy the ranch, encourage an offer...*any offer*. Just get a contract. Even if it comes in lower than we discussed, it's not like I can't get a job in the city. I've never shied away from work, and don't plan on starting any time soon." He'd do anything to get the place sold, including selling for less than what it was worth.

"Are you sure?" Paul asked.

"Sell the place. I found a place in Dallas, but they won't hold it much longer for me." Not to mention he'd lose the deposit, money he couldn't afford to waste. Wishful thinking had him moving forward to his new life faster than had been wise.

Chapter Two

♥

THE COWBOY HAD PUT Diana in her place soundly, even if slightly unwarranted. Or maybe totally warranted. The idea of a bull charging them was not something she had considered. But then, who kept a bull in an open pasture with a fence that needed mending? The property was gorgeous, what she'd seen of it anyway. As she drove past the driveway that most likely led to the ranch, her gaze landed on another one of the for-sale signs.

"Mommy, I really need to go bad," Lindsey said.

"Okay, sweetie. Mommy is doing the best she can." The woods would have worked just fine if it hadn't been for the cowboy bent on moving them off the property. Diana hadn't always been a city girl, and when the need arose, one took care of business. Suddenly she laid on the brakes and backed the vehicle up. Houses on the market had bathrooms, not to mention she was more than a little curious about the farmhouse. The views had to be incredible with sweeping pastures framed out by the mountains in the distance.

Diana called the number on the sign, hoping the realtor was available. If not, maybe even a lockbox code would get them inside and she could check the place out privately. *Assuming the owner wasn't home.*

"Mayberry Realty. This is Paul. How can I help you?"

"I'm calling about the farm for sale on SR29 in Crossroads Creek. Are you the realtor handling the listing?" Diana asked.

"I am. That's the Thompson place. I take it you'd like to see it?"

Boy, would she. The house and the bathroom specifically, but Diana didn't plan to share that much information. "I would love to. Is there a lockbox code or something I could use to get in? I mean, if the owner isn't around, of course."

"Nothing like that, sorry. This is the country and I'm never far away. When would you like to meet up?" he asked.

"Now." *Five minutes ago.*

"Well, okay then. I'll head that way. Just sit tight and I'll be there in about ten minutes."

Too long, judging by her daughter's strained look and dancing in her booster seat. "Listen, is there any chance there's a key somewhere and we can go inside to wait for you? I promise not to touch anything." Except the bathroom, that is. *Truth time.* "The thing is...my six-year-old daughter really needs to go to the bathroom.

If you've ever had children, you would understand."

"Oh, I've got three girls and two boys. And yes, I'm quite familiar with emergency status ratings on bathroom calls. Feel free to go inside. I just talked to the owner, and he's not at home. Go on in, the house is unlocked and I'll be right along."

Diana let out a sigh of relief. It was all very odd, but a blessing in disguise. "Thank you so much. I'll see you in a few minutes." She hung up, eager to get Lindsey inside. Diana drove the rest of the way down the driveway and, upon clearing the last bend, she was more than a little surprised at what she saw. The pristine farm house she'd imagined in her head couldn't be further from the truth. The house needed a good coat of paint, but otherwise, it was inviting and warm. Rockers lined the front porch and she could almost picture the neighbors coming over for tea. "Come on, sweetheart," she said, ushering her daughter out of the car and up the front steps.

"Who lives here, Mommy? Are we tres...tres-passing again?" she asked, getting the big word right.

Hand on the door knob, she paused. It was a bit out of the ordinary to just walk into someone's house, but duty called. Pushing open the door, she peeked inside just to be sure the place was vacant. "I don't know, but the house is for sale and I want to look at it. Wouldn't it be love-ly to own those beautiful bluebonnet fields?" she offered, trying to redirect her daughter's thoughts. They weren't trespassing since tech-nically they had permission, but it was a com-plicated discussion and the bathroom stop took precedence.

"Oh, yes. If I had a horse like his, I could just ride forever. As long as the nasty, mean bull isn't around," Lindsey added, her face scrunched up tight.

Wooden floors and outdated furniture filled the place, but at least it was clean. Spotless almost. Pictures and Knick knacks filled the shelves. The house needed a good airing out as well, a slightly musty odor clinging to the air. First things first, then she'd come back and take a closer look. "I'm sure there's a bathroom down this way." Diana led her daughter down the hall and sure enough, the first door was exactly what they needed. "I'll wait for you out here. Be sure to wash your hands."

"Yes, Mommy. I always do," Lindsey quipped.

Her sweet daughter had a touch of independence developing, reminding Diana of herself at that age. While waiting, she couldn't resist poking her head in the first bedroom, her curiosity in overdrive. She flipped on the light and glanced around, shocked to see a wedding dress laid out on the bed. The dress explained a lot about the place. A woman's touch was obvious with some of the artificial flower arrangements and pretty landscape paintings that hung on the walls of the hall. Perhaps the owner just got married and his new wife wasn't much into farming. Which might be the best thing possible for Diana and her daughter because the more she thought about it, the more the idea of buying the place held appeal. There was something about the house that felt right...like a home. Something she and her daughter desperately needed to find.

After weeks of driving and checking out various towns as they drifted around the country, Crossroads Creek and the farm appealed in a way no other place had. And it would be the last place her ex-husband would come looking for them. *In other words, perfect.*

She returned to the bathroom just as her daughter came out, still drying her hands on her jeans, proof she'd washed them. Even if she wasn't drying them properly.

"There's the prettiest picture of a little girl in the bathroom. She's on a horse and looks so happy. I wonder who it is?" Lindsey asked.

Diana shrugged. "I don't know. Maybe the owner has children. Or it could be a niece or nephew." More than likely, it wasn't something they would find out, as the private lives of people selling their homes wasn't exactly a welcome discussion. The man from earlier today was wrong. Privacy was big no matter whether you lived in the city or in the country.

"I wish I could ride a horse. If we buy this place, can I get a horse? Please, Mommy," she pleaded. Her daughter turned pitiful blue eyes up at her, knowing it was her best chance to get what she wanted. With all that Lindsey had been through, Diana was a softie for most things. Anything to make her daughter happy. Just not this. *At least not now.*

"Let's just agree to check out the house at this point. No sense crossing bridges that lead nowhere." It was something Grandma Rose used to say. Diana's heart ached with the need for her grandmother's loving arms and support, especially with all the recent changes in her life. Rose Langley had been her rock, while Diana's parents had been the boat that set her adrift in a stormy sea. Luckily, Virginia and Dave Reston no longer controlled Diana's life and her decisions.

They stepped inside the first bedroom, Diana's gaze instantly going to the gorgeous white wedding gown she'd noticed earlier.

"*Oooh*, look at this, Mommy." Lindsey darted over to the bed and gently touched the silky fabric. What a beautiful wedding dress. Don't you think so, Mommy?"

"I do. The bride was a very lucky lady."

"Someday, I want to wear one just like this," Lindsey exclaimed, her face wreathed in a warm glowing smile.

"And you will look simply lovely for your handsome husband," Diana said, smiling at her daughter. Lindsey had been more focused lately on dreams of the future, perhaps finding it more appealing than dealing with her parents' shortcomings.

Little girls loved to dream of their wedding, and Diana hadn't been any different. At least, not until her parents put an end to any fanciful notions she might have had. By the time Diana was sixteen, she'd known the future mapped out for her.

Illusion Electronics was a global company, with Silas Gibson as half heir to the business, and Diana the other half. The result was an arranged marriage between her and Silas. It was a plan devised to guarantee the future of the company the four parents founded together and had grown into a multi-billion-dollar business. Forced to choose between being set adrift without a penny, her helicopter parents had ensured her compliance. And it might have all turned out okay if it hadn't been for Silas's gambling addiction or his wandering eyes that led him down a sinful road that disrespected every fiber of their wedding vows.

Lindsey flitted around the room. "And I love the pink and lace of the bedroom. If we get the place, I get dibs on this room. And you don't have to change a thing."

"Don't touch anything. We are just here to look," Diana admonished. "Come on, let's go see the rest of the house." Hand in hand, they moved down the hall, checking out the master suite. It was basic at best. Functional was a good word. Sturdy bed and dresser. No pictures or decorations of any sort. Of course, the muddy cowboy boots and jeans and plaid shirt on the floor in the corner explained everything. It would seem the new bride didn't have domain over the man's bedroom. Not yet.

Diana admired the couple had clearly been old-fashioned.

A simple life without all the trappings of the city. No fake birthday parties. No social parties that looked like a who's who of the business world. This is what she wanted for her daughter. "Let's go check out the kitchen. I think I just heard the front door shut, so the realtor must be here. I've got lots of questions for him," Diana said, eager to leave the room and the odd sense of trespassing in someone's personal space.

She headed out the door, slamming into a hard wall of chest, Lindsey tumbling into her from behind as progress halted. "*Oomph.*" Diana shot her hand out to grab the doorway, connecting with the man's well-chiseled biceps instead. "Oh, my goodness. I'm so..." She looked up, words failing her. Dark brown eyes bore into hers.

It was the cowboy from earlier this afternoon—the one who had thrown them off the property.

"You seem to have a habit of showing up where you don't belong. Is there a reason you're snooping through my bedroom?" he asked, his eyes glancing around the room and then landing on Lindsey before returning to her.

"We're...we're meeting Paul. The realtor," she added to explain. Not that it was needed. "You're not Paul, are you?" she asked, ruling out the most obvious explanation that seemed pretty farfetched.

"No, I'm not Paul. I'm Chad Thompson. The *owner* of the ranch and the house you're in."

The owner? Diana was more than interested in the farm, but she'd gotten off to a rocky start with the man who held the key to any chance she had of buying the place. The cowboy glaring down at her would more than likely not sell to her on principal alone. The principal of the fact she'd been caught trespassing...twice. Although, the second time, she had permission, so it didn't count.

"I'm Diana Gi...Langley," she said, catching herself before she let slip her married name. The name she ditched after the divorce and taking her grandmother's last name. She offered her hand in a greeting.

They shook, the warmth of his calloused hand matching the power in his grip.

"Hello, anyone in here?" a male voice called out from the front room.

"Down here. It would seem there's a party in my bedroom," Chad said, a disgruntled expression marring his face. "This," Chad said, jerking his thumb toward the balding man coming down the hall, "is Paul. Next time, how about not letting people into my personal space without you to show them around?"

Paul shrugged, not at all intimidated by the cowboy. "The kid had to go to the bathroom. Lighten up," he said, coming to their defense, and not at all intimidated by the hulking brute. "They're harmless, not to mention you want buyers to see the place. Right?"

Chad shook his head. "Sure thing. I'll leave you to show them around. Maybe there's parts of the house they haven't seen." Chad tipped his hat and walked away. The handsome cowboy wore a bad attitude like a well-fitted shirt. *Tailor made.*

"Don't mind him. He's not exactly the sociable kind of guy," Paul said.

Diana could have guessed that much on her own. And after Silas, anti-social looked pretty darn good...or it would if she was interested...which she wasn't. One failed marriage was enough to last her a lifetime. Silas's poor character qualities had infinitely sped up the demise of the marriage, the ending faster than the horses he loved to bet on at the track. A love that extended to other women and did not include his wife and daughter.

Money was Silas's ticket, and unfortunately, Diana had plenty. It was also the reason she was now considering buying the farm. It was a place far from New York City, a place where, hopefully, Silas would never find her. He had blackmailed her once, using the custody of his daughter as leverage for money. *Never again.*

An hour later, there hadn't been so much as a glimpse of the owner. The place needed work, but she had the time to fix it up, and the money to make it happen. Not that she would let a soul in Crossroads Creek know about her financial status. They were here to leave the past behind, something she could only do if the money trail that led to her door disappeared.

Diana prayed for guidance, hoping for some sign this was the right place for her and Lindsey. A new home. As she walked around the house again, a sense of peace filled her. Peace that came from God. *A peace she trusted.*

"So, what do you think?" Paul asked as he and Lindsey rejoined her.

"I love it. I'm curious though...why is the place in such a state of disrepair? Is there a problem in the dairy industry I should know about?"

Paul's lips thinned as he considered her questions. "Truth is that dairy farming is highly competitive. Small operations are going out of business left and right. It doesn't help that Chad's buyers have to travel further to get here, which cuts into how much fresh milk he can provide. The place needs to grow and to modernize if it's going to succeed."

"Explain what you meant about the buyers traveling further. I don't understand," Diana said, more than a little confused.

"*Ummm,* the problem is...Chad only deals with buyers in Wylie and Fontana. Nothing local."

"Why?" It was like pulling teeth to get the realtor to explain.

"That's a question you would need to ask Chad. None of my business and it's personal."

"I see. Sort of. If it's personal, it won't stop me from selling local so that's a hurdle I can handle. But there's one other major setback I can foresee. I have an idea how to make it work through the issue, but it's not ideal." After checking out the barn and what she could see of the property and glancing over the listing details, Diana knew she was getting in over her head. Not financially...but in knowledge and skills.

"What's that?" The realtor's eyes had a sudden glow, the man sensing a sale and, therefore, a commission.

"How agreeable do you think the owner will be in negotiating the contract?"

Paul nodded. "Very. He's looking to sell sooner rather than later. Name your price and I'll see if we can't get him to agree," he added eagerly.

Diana was pretty sure a place in this condition wouldn't sell easy, and it was a buyer's market. Except her price had nothing to do with money, and everything to do with the man.

"Let me think this over tonight and I'll get back to you first thing in the morning," Diana said, already knowing in her heart the right answer.

But she wouldn't rush such an important decision. Silas had been one big mistake and she vowed not to make another.

Chapter Three

♥

CHAD WIPED THE SWEAT from his brow, then picked up the sledgehammer, landing strike after strike on the metal post as he drove it into the ground. Satisfied, he picked up another post and moved to the next stake. Eight down and twenty-two to go before sunset if he wanted to finish repairing the chicken pen.

Chimes broke the silence of the stifling heat and he pulled his phone out of his back pocket. "Chad," he said, not paying much attention to who was calling. He had work to do and chatting on the phone wouldn't get it done.

"You need to come to my office right away. You've got an offer on the property," Paul said, the excitement in his voice unmistakable.

"Well, I'll be a dancing chicken." Clearly, he had chickens on the brain for such a lame comment to come out of his mouth. "The woman?" Chad asked, knowing buyers were slim pickings he was happily shocked at the turn of events.

"Yes, and her name is Diana. She's here now and would like to move forward with a contract." Paul sounded sure of himself. Too sure.

Although Chad had told him to sell at any price, maybe he shouldn't have given the man that much freedom. "Must be an excellent offer, considering we aren't discussing terms."

"You said sell the property, and that's what I'm doing. Are you going to keep talking or get yourself down here to sign before she comes to her senses and changes her mind?"

"I'm on my way." Chad tossed his tools back into the truck and hopped in. He turned around and headed for town, still more than a little surprised at the news. It was something he'd been looking forward to for years, and now that the time was upon him, it took some getting used to.

He glanced around, the farm land familiar...every nuance of it. There were some things he'd miss, but not the blood, sweat, and frustrations that came with it. He couldn't help but wonder what price Paul had negotiated, hoping enough that when he moved to Dallas, he'd be able to afford some creature comforts and plenty of time to relax before he had to find another job.

Downtime was as foreign to him as understanding women. The plan was to change the first, but stay far away from the second. Ever since Tonia left him for the bright lights of the city and another man, Chad didn't see any reason to invest in another relationship. Waste of time if you asked him.

Time he might have now, with freedom just around the corner.

Seven minutes later, he parked in front of the realtor's office. Grabbing his hat off the front seat, he jammed it low on his head and headed inside, the overhead bell jingling to announce his arrival.

Lindsey looked up from where she sat on the couch, but immediately went back to her coloring book. It would seem he hadn't made any friends yesterday, but then he probably deserved the cold-shoulder treatment given how unyielding he'd been with them. At least it hadn't stopped Diana from wanting to buy the farm, but seriously, how could he have known?

Paul came into the room, his smile and upbeat attitude a given. "Glad to see you could make it, Chad. Exciting day for everyone. Although you do seem to carry a stench," he said, his face scrunched up. "You could have stopped to wash up, my friend. Sweat isn't conducive to a good impression."

Chad didn't begrudge the commission to his lifelong friend, but his comment was over the top. "Stick to selling my property. I'm not interested in making a good impression, so sweat or no sweat, show me where to sign."

"If you say so." Paul shrugged. "Diana is in the conference room and she's already signed the contracts. There's just a few little things we need to discuss regarding the deal. Once you sign, we can move forward with the process."

"Sounds great." Chad followed him and the two men joined Diana.

"Nice to see you again," she said, a half-smile, half-smirk on her face.

She hadn't forgotten their auspicious meeting yesterday any more than he had, but in this case, he would give her the advantage, considering she was following through with her declaration to buy the farm. "Likewise. Sorry about yesterday. I hadn't realized you were truly interested in the place. I'm glad you like the farm." It was lame as far as apologies went, but definitely due.

"Like? I wouldn't buy a place I liked. I love it. The wide-open land, smell of fresh air and sunshine...what's not to love? The house and barn need work, but it's a home. Which is exactly what Lindsey and I are looking for, without the complications and craziness of the city."

"*Hmmphh.* You and I are two totally different people. I want exactly what you don't. Too bad we couldn't trade houses or whatever it is people do when they want to trade places."

"That's usually vacation places and people swap. But trust me, you don't want what I had." Diana spoke with such disdain he couldn't help but wonder what type of housing she'd lived in, although his guess would be not much given what little he knew about her and the old Buick she drove.

Although her stylish hair and manicured nails and clothes said differently. Perhaps the truth was she was all about the outward show to others, hoping to improve her lot in life. The farm wasn't any place for the city girl, but there was no way he wouldn't sell it to her. A buyer was a buyer, no matter whether they understood what they were getting into. "I guess we'll have to agree to disagree. So where do I sign?" he asked, picking up one of the ten plus pens scattered on the table.

"Not so fast," Paul said, suddenly looking a little less sure of himself. "You need to look over the offer first," he added, sliding a stack of papers across the table.

Chad's gaze immediately went to the bottom-line number he wanted to see. *Full price.* This was better than anything he could have expected. *So what was the problem?* "Looks good to me." Better than good, as visions of going out on the town flashed through his brain.

"There's a contingency. I'll let Diana explain as it's a bit unorthodox," Paul said, sitting back in his leather chair and turning his attention to the new buyer.

"Whatever you want, I'm fine with it." Chad shrugged. "Full price can get you a lot of bonuses. What do you need? Help with closing costs. Extra time for your husband to get here and see the property or to get the loan in place. Name it." He was beside himself with relief, his financial woes soon to be a thing of the past.

Diana rolled her eyes, a secret look passing between her and Paul. Chad had a feeling he wasn't going to like whatever she had to say.

"First off, there is no husband. Second, I don't need help with the financial aspect as I've got approval for the funds in place already. What I need is you."

Surely he hadn't heard her right. Was this some sort of joke? "Come again? I don't think I understood what you said."

"You heard right. I need you." Color suffused her pretty cheeks, turning them a bright pink. "To *help* me with the farm, that is."

"No." He was selling the farm...not himself.

Diana stood. She brushed a hand through her hair, almost as though she were a little nervous. "You haven't heard my offer." Her voice was steady, in direct contrast to the insecure move she seemed to not know was a giveaway to her actual emotions.

What she was asking wasn't possible. "I don't need to hear it. I'm sorry. My plan is to move to the city. The whole reason I'm selling is to get away from the farm and everything it represents."

Diana leaned forward on the table, her hands planted firmly in front of him. "I'm not asking you to give up your dreams, even if I don't agree with them. I'm asking you to help me for the next thirty days while the farm goes through the closing process. It takes time to do the inspections, the title search, and to get through the paperwork. Thirty days...that's all I want from you."

Chad was missing something in the exchange. "Exactly what do you need me for?" he asked, trying to clarify.

"To teach me how to be a dairy farmer."

Chad coughed and shook his head. This was beyond anything he could have expected. "You mean to tell me you're buying a dairy farm and don't know the first thing about a cow and how to do the milking?" There was no way he could sell the property to her. As much as he wanted out, he still wanted the place to succeed. Someone to restore the farm to its former glory.

"Hilarious, wise guy. I'm not a total idiot when it comes to living in the country. But dairy farming is more than just living on the land. I want you to teach me about the cattle, the horses, and any other animals here. What they eat, what they need from me, what I need to repair and keep up. Information on buyers and vets, and what the cows need by way of medicine to stay healthy. Basically, all the ins and outs of a dairy farm. I'm a fast learner."

"This is ridiculous." Chad leaned back in the chair and shook his head, glaring at Diana, and then at Paul.

"You can always say no and wait for another buyer." Diana's comment was delivered with a confidence he hadn't expected.

"She's right," Paul chimed in. "Buyers are beating down your door and you can probably expect another offer in, say, six months to a year. Maybe more."

"I can do without the sarcasm, and I'm well aware of the situation." Chad ran a hand through his hair. "Do you see me? Really see me. I'm sweaty and covered in dirt. This is what the life looks like most of the time. Why would you want this?" It was a fair question and one he expected her to answer.

"I'm well aware it's hard work. And as to why…I consider that none of your business," Diana said, her chin going up a notch.

The woman liked her privacy, something she wouldn't get in Crossroads Creek. She'd find out soon enough…if he sold to her. It's not like he really had much choice in the matter, not if he wanted out of Crossroads Creek. Besides, it's not like he could just up and walk away from working the place until the deal closed and had the money in hand. The problem was Diana wanted to be his sidekick. "And what about your daughter? While you're playing tag along, what will she be doing?" He was trying to get her to see reason, because if she didn't back down on this contingency, Chad was going to accept. Giving her every opportunity to change her mind seemed only fair.

"I'll be registering her in school come Monday morning," Diana said, her confidence growing with each minute that passed.

"I see. And where do you expect to live?"

Diana frowned. "Not at the farm, if that's what you're asking. That wouldn't be the right message to send Lindsey, and I wouldn't want anyone to get the wrong idea."

Perhaps she understood more about small-town gossip than Chad gave her credit.

"There's a nice bed-and-breakfast right here in town called Serendipity. Janice Edwin is a wonderful woman, and I'm sure she's got a room available," Paul offered.

"That sounds lovely. I'll check on that when we're finished here. We have a deal, don't we?" Her gaze never left him as she waited for the answer.

"Sure. Thirty days max." And at the end of the thirty days, if Diana wanted to run back to the city and her hair and nail appointments, Chad would still have her under contract.

The dairy farm would be her problem—not his.

Chapter Four

♥

"Lindsey," Diana called out, glancing at her watch. They were behind schedule as the school office opened at eight. She had planned to get in and get out with the registration process, knowing Chad was expecting her at the ranch for her first day of training. And Diana still needed to make a quick stop at the five and dime store for some essentials. Like boots. Perhaps regular jeans versus the designer ones she sported at the moment. Not to mention a couple of extra shirts, preferably a few plaid ones that said country through and through and helped her to blend in with the locals.

Anything that wouldn't draw attention to Lindsey or herself. The art of getting lost involved lying low and Diana planned to play the part to perfection. Their future depended on it.

"Lindsey," she called again, gathering up her purse and keys. Her daughter had been withdrawn this morning, not in the least interested in going to school and making new friends. She had made it clear on several occasions that her preference was spending the day at the farm with Diana.

It wasn't possible for a multitude of reasons, but a six-year-old wasn't interested in reasons the answer was no. Lindsey only wanted to hear a yes. Diana made her way to the small bedroom they shared at the inn, each room having its own sitting area and bathroom. With no sign of her daughter, she checked the bathroom. "Come on, Lindsey. We need to leave." She hadn't seen her daughter in over ten minutes, and their room wasn't large enough to get lost. A rush of anxiety had her nerves shooting into overdrive. "Lindsey, please answer me. You're starting to worry me."

"I don't want to go to school." The quiet voice came from the bedroom.

Diana headed back that way, relieved her daughter was still here. "Sweetheart, it will be fun. Trust me. You'll meet new kids and make friends." She got down on her hands and knees to check under the bed, the only place she hadn't looked. *Bingo.*

A sniffling sob escaped. "I had friends at my other school. I miss them," her daughter said, sniffling again.

The sound was heart wrenching. "I know, and we talked about this. It's just you and me now, kiddo. We have a chance to start over. Think of this as an adventure. This is just the beginning, and I need you to trust me. And after we move to the farm, think of all the fun you can have. And you can have a horse and learn to ride." Diana wasn't above using the ace in the hole, even if it meant putting her daughter on a horse sooner than she'd planned if it would help during the change.

"Really?" Lindsey asked, her voice going higher with a twinge of excitement.

Diana nodded. "Yes. But fun also comes with responsibility, and right now, that means school." *The art of compromise.*

"Okay," Lindsey murmured, sliding out from under the bed.

Already late leaving, this set them back further, but it was the best Diana could do. She gave Lindsey a hug. "Good choice. Now let's get going. If we want to be dairy farmers, I've got to learn how." Diana laughed.

"I'm going to be a farmer?" Lindsey asked.

"You are." They climbed into the car and Diana pulled out onto the main road to head for the school.

"Goody. But what's a farmer got to do? I mean is it like Old Mr. McDonald who had a farm. He had pigs, and goats, and chickens, and ducks. I can't remember the rest of the song." Her face was drawn up tight as she thought it over.

Better to set Lindsey straight right away. "Farmers can be many things. They are people who own a lot of land, but sometimes they farm the land for crops. Others for dairy cows. Ranchers raise cattle for meat or horses to ride and race. And sometimes, there are other animals that live on the farm, but that varies from place to place."

"So we won't have lots of horses since we're farmers?"

"Something like that," Diana said, grinning over at her daughter as they pulled into the parking lot. "We only need what we can ride."

"Oh, okay. I just want one anyway." Lindsey's winning smile was a surefire sign her daughter had it all figured out in her head.

Parking in one of the front guest parking spaces, they headed up the sidewalk toward the entrance. The school was fairly new, the building brick and modern. Lush green lawns and bushes in bloom welcomed students to their happy place for the day.

"May I help you?" a greeter asked at the door.

Diana was pleased they had some sort of security at the school. "Yes. I'm here to register my daughter as we are new in town. Which way to the administrative offices?"

"That's the door you see there," the woman said, pointing a little way down the hall and to the right. "Here's a pass to show I cleared you to enter." The woman scratched some info on a pink slip of paper and handed it to her.

"Thank you." Diana could feel Lindsey's hesitation as they drew close, her fears resurfacing. They entered the office and sat down to wait for the secretary to return, the sign on her desk alerting them she'd stepped away for a few minutes.

Several people came and went before a smiling woman came through the door. Dressed in a skirted suit of navy blue, it was only her flowery blouse that added a touch of fun to the business outfit. And her heels were functional, not flattering. Luckily, Diana wouldn't need anything for an office setting. Serviceable would be her new operative word.

The woman dropped a stack of papers on her desk before turning to officially greet her visitors. "Sorry to keep you waiting. Mornings are always the busiest trying to get the kids settled into their homerooms. How can I help you?"

"No problem." Diana's busy schedule wasn't the woman's issue. "We've recently arrived from New York and went under contract to buy a farm near here. I'd like to get Lindsey back in school so she can finish out first grade."

"Certainly. And welcome to Crossroads Creek. Are you talking about the Thompson farm? I hadn't heard it sold," the woman asked, eyeing her with a more intensified gaze.

"We only signed the paperwork yesterday. I'm staying at the Serendipity until the closing."

"I see. Well congratulations, I think. That place needs a lot of work. Is your husband with you?" the woman asked, pushing her glasses back on her nose before her gaze drifted down to Diana's left hand.

"Ex-husband. And no. It's going to be just Lindsey and I, and the wide-open space of the farm."

"Wow. I'm impressed. And you from New York City. Quite the change. You've got your work cut out for you, as the place has fallen into a state of disrepair over the past couple of years. But I'm guessing you know all that, seeing as your buying the place. Will be nice to see the farm brought back up to speed."

"What happened to it?" Diana asked, unable to curb her curiosity.

The woman frowned. "I guess you could say a lot of things, most of it in a long ago past. More recently, I think Chad Thompson has had one boot out the door, so to speak. Now that his sister got married and moved to town, I don't think Chad's heart is tied to the land anymore. And then with his girlfriend of two years up and leaving him for another man to head for the city because she wasn't cut out for "living in the sticks" didn't help any. Her words, not mine. And then there's the fact he's forced to sell his milk to the processors in Wylie and Fontana." The woman lowered her voice as she spoke, glancing around as if to be reassured no one else had heard.

"Why doesn't he sell locally?" Diana shouldn't encourage the woman, but information about what she was walking into was key. Information Paul was reluctant to share.

"I've probably said more than I should already. Just saying he does. Doubt you'll have the same problem."

The woman's comments were all too similar to what Paul had told her. "Well, that's good." It was obvious the secretary was past sharing confidences and ready to do business as she handed Diana a folder with a stack of papers to fill out.

"Just fill out all the forms in this package. If you'd like, I can take Lindsey to her class and introduce her. I'll get her old school to send over a transcript. Not that first grade is much of a record other than to certify her attendance." The woman rose and came around the desk.

"I brought a copy if you'd like one," Diana said, reaching into her purse to retrieve the envelope. Allison had got one with a new last name for Lindsey before they left the city.

The woman took the document and checked it over. She rubbed a finger over the seal mark, a frown marring her face. "Thanks, but we can't use this as an official record. It must have a raised seal to make it official, not a copy. Copies can be altered. I hope you understand."

Diana hadn't thought about an official copy and it definitely presented a problem. How did one leave the past behind and start over if you had to connect the dots? Dots her ex-husband wouldn't lose time in following if it led to the money. *Her money.* Silas didn't care about Lindsey, only using a custody battle threat as leverage to get more money he didn't deserve. "I see. Lindsey, are you okay to go with...*ummm*, I didn't catch your name," she said, looking up at the woman.

"Sorry. Veronica Bradley. Administrator to the Principal over Parkview Elementary."

"Nice to meet you. I'm Diana Langley." Another pang of doubt hit her square in the gut. Her married name had been Gibson, and it was the name on the records back in New York City. She had to try again. "If I can get this copy certified, can you accept it? I would prefer not to, *ummm*, have the past follow us here, if you know what I mean?" It was opening up a small window into a past she preferred no one to know but getting Lindsey into school was more important.

Veronica nodded, shooting her a friendly wink. "Say no more, honey. When there's an ex involved, stuff happens. Trust me, I know. If you can get it certified, it'll cover my end of the record keeping."

Diana inhaled and then let out a deep breath, the relief dizzying. "Thank you so much for understanding." She kneeled down by Lindsey. "Sweetheart, do you want to go with Ms. Bradley? Meet the kids and see what you think. I'm sure you'll make new friends."

Her daughter clutched her hand, unwilling to let go. "But where will you be if I don't like them?" she asked, her eyes wide in fear.

"I'll be at the farm. And Ms. Bradley will call if you need to reach me, okay? Remember, we talked about this." She brushed Lindsey's hair back from her face and gave her daughter a kiss on the forehead.

Veronica held out her hand and smiled. "You're going to love it here, I promise. Let's see, I think Maddie and Marie, two of the girls in your class, would love to meet you. They're twins, but also fairly new to the area. And the other kids are friendly and you'll have no problem fitting in."

Lindsey's eyes glazed over with tears. "Okay. But I still don't think I'll like it. It's scary coming to a new school. And I liked my other friends." Her lower lip trembled as she fought back against crying.

"Be a big girl. And I'll pick you up from school at three, right out in front of the building. Then you can tell me all about the fun day you had." Diana prayed the day would go well as it would make life that much easier for them both.

"*Okayyy.*" She took Veronica's hand, and the two walked out of the office, leaving Diana to fill out the forms.

It broke her heart to see her daughter upset at the changes, but they were necessary, even if she couldn't explain them to Lindsey. Diana glanced at her watch. So much for fashionably late. More like Chad would think she was a no show...or that she had changed her mind. Something he wouldn't mind one bit.

Not a chance.

She filled out the forms, careful to only include her new last name. Using her grandmother's last name had been a stroke of genius, especially since it was the trust account her grandmother left her that enabled Diana to break free of Silas and her parents. It's not that she didn't love her parents, and she'd give anything to change the way things were. But it had been their decisions to arrange her marriage to Silas in the first place, and their decision to threaten to cut her off if she hadn't married the man.

Business partners looking to merge on a more permanent level, making it a family business. Young and naïve, she'd finally given in. There was never any love between them, but she had hoped they could be friends. Except the world didn't know Silas the way she did. The Golden Boy everyone loved had an alter ego life no one knew existed. *Except her.* Not that anyone would have believed her.

And then there was Lindsey to think about. Outing Silas would serve no purpose except to hurt her daughter. No matter what, Silas was still her father, even if the man was stupid enough not to want anything to do with his sweet little girl.

Diana finished filling out the forms and laid them on the desk just as Veronica arrived. "Did everything go okay?"

Veronica did one of those odd nodding shakes of the head. Which stood for so-so.

Not good enough, but for a first day Diana would have to see where it led.

Veronica picked up the file and glanced inside. "Lindsey's skittish, but given time, I think she'll be all right. Some kids take a little more time to adjust than others," she added, trying to reassure Diana.

"I'll talk to her again. Thank you. I've got a friend who can get a certified copy and express mail it to me. I've got to run, but I'll be back at three to pick up Lindsey. Call me if she needs me...for anything."

As she made her way to the car, Diana couldn't help but wonder about the decision to buy the farm. Had she made the right choice? Would the folks in Crossroads Creek welcome her and Lindsey into the mix, allowing them to make a life here?

Stopping at the five and dime, she made short order of picking out new serviceable clothes and boots. After changing in the dressing room, she stepped back to check out her appearance. The look differed completely from her fancier city clothes, the boots stiff, the cotton of the shirt scratchy, but at least the jeans fit well and were more than a little comfortable as compared to the designer ones she'd worn into the store.

On the way to the Thompson place, she called Allison to set the wheels in motion for the school records. It had been a narrow escape and Diana wanted to tidy up the loose ends. Friends since kindergarten, it was Allison who had tried to talk her out of marrying Silas in the first place. But the parental pressure had been too much. She should have listened to her friend. But then she wouldn't have Lindsey, and her daughter made everything worthwhile.

"Hey, you. I'm so glad you called. I've been worried. Where are you?" Allison asked when she answered. Her friend had the worry-wort character down to an art form.

"I'm fine. We're fine. Are you in a private place to chat?" Diana asked, not willing to take chances Allison would be overheard, considering she worked as an administrator for the family business Diana had just left behind. Allison was her eyes and ears about what was happening at Illusions Electronics.

"I am. Sally just went on lunch break," she said, her voice dropping lower.

"Oh, that's right. I forgot about the time change. So I've got to make this quick as I've got an appointment with a cowboy as of about thirty minutes ago."

"Whoa. Let's start with the most important part of that comment. Tell me about the cowboy Miss I've-Sworn-Off-Men?"

Diana smiled. Her friend was way off base, but a little fun never hurt. "Tall, good looking, wavy brown hair, and dark chocolate eyes. Drool worthy," she teased.

"Stop. We know that's only in the movies. He must be short, bald, and have sappy eyes." Allison laughed.

"Or somewhere in between." *Liar*. Her first description was spot on, but sidetracking Allison on the subject was a good thing. "Anyway, I'm in Texas. And...I bought a dairy farm. Or I'm buying one, anyway."

"You've got to be kidding me. You're not a farmer," Allison exclaimed.

"I know. That's where the cowboy comes in. Who better to teach me what I need to know than the guy who owns the place and is selling?" It had been a genius idea, even if it had taken a little strong arming the guy into agreeing.

"Have you lost your mind?"

Diana chuckled. "Not at all. Or at least I hope not. I hope I've found our new home and a place we can be happy with none of the past to weigh us down." It was the same thing she prayed for every morning. Surely this had been the answer to those prayers.

"Got to hand it to you girl, when you do something, it's all in or nothing. Anyway, I've got lots to tell you about what's going on here."

Diana drove down the driveway and pulled up next to the house. "It'll have to wait. I just arrived at the farm for my first instructional day and judging by the look on Chad's face, the man's not a happy camper."

"Happy cowboy," Allison teased.

"Or that. Listen, the school needs a certified copy of the form you got for me. Can you see your way to making it happen? Just be careful. We need to make sure no one knows what you're up to, or why. And then I'll get you the address of the place I'm staying and you can overnight it to me." She trusted Allison would be discreet, but reminders never hurt.

"I'll take care of it. And don't worry, this isn't my first rodeo dealing with the likes of Silas and all the parentals. Just because they're my bosses, doesn't mean they own me."

"Unlike they did with me," Diana ground out. "But it's good to know, not that I ever doubted you. And please, don't start with the country cowboy terminology. I have a feeling I'm about to be inundated with it. Thanks, Allison. I'll call again and we can chat longer as soon as I have some free time now that Lindsey's in school." She especially needed to hear what was going on back in the city, but it would have to wait until tonight.

The two hung up and Diana slid out of the car.

"Nice to see you could finally show up. Does this mean you've changed your mind?" Chad asked, almost a little too hopefully.

"Not a chance, cowboy." Her priorities were God, Lindsey, and then the farm. And nowhere on that list was Chad Thompson.

Chapter Five

♥

CHAD HAD ALREADY LOST valuable time while keeping a watch out for Diana. "Your priorities seem a little out of whack," he said, wishing he could end this situation before it even started.

"It's called a register-your-daughter-for-school morning. You're right, life *is* about priorities, and Lindsey's mine. The farm comes second, or it will after the closing." She crossed her arms in defiance, unwilling to back down.

He admired her can-do attitude, but this was over the top. "This whole contingency of yours seems somewhat ridiculous, if you ask me. Do you even know the first thing about dairy farming or dairy cattle?" Even her boots, jeans, and shirt spelled new experience, although the tag that still clung to the leg of the jeans removed all doubt. Her feet would hurt come morning for sure.

Diana's answering smile could almost be labeled a smirk. "The first thing, yes. The second and third...no. That's what you're for."

Chad shook his head. "Fine. Let's start at the beginning. Do you know how to ride a horse?" he asked, prepared for the worst, and hoping for the best. It would make things somewhat easier if she had some fundamentals of life in the country, on a farm, no less.

She shrugged. "Yes, and no."

"Do you ever answer questions straight up?"

"Sometimes." Diana shot him a grin. "I used to ride when I was a kid. My grandmother had a ranch, so although I was too young to understand much of what was going on around me, I learned to ride and I have been on a ranch for a few summers. The problem is my time there ended when I was ten and I haven't ridden at all since then. Unless you count my guided trail rides on horses more content to make their way back to the barn than any genuine interest in a ride."

He let out a sigh of relief. They had a starting point, which was more than he had ten minutes ago. "Those don't count. But riding a horse is like riding a bike. Sounds like you'll be fine, and I've picked out a fairly docile mare for you to ride. I've already milked the cows this morning, so I thought we'd start by checking fences, knowing it will give you a chance to see the entire property. You didn't waste time going under contract, and it might be good for you to see what makes the place special." Since this woman was all-fire determined to buy the farm, Chad would see to it as much as possible she was prepared. A month wasn't much time.

"I'll trust you to know what's best for me to learn and in what order. You're the boss for the next thirty days."

Chad led her to the barn, where he had his horse and another mare waiting. "I saddled the horses to save time since you were late. On a dairy farm, schedules are important. And even though I'm down to fifty cows, they still need a lot of attention and care and regularly sched-uled milking times." He untied the reins and handed them to Diana. "This is Firefly. She's well-trained and will know what to do, even if you aren't so sure."

"Look, I'm sorry I was late. Can we put that behind us and start over? Otherwise, this is going to be a long month," Diana asked, not making any move to get on the horse.

It was going to be a long month no matter how they proceeded, but Diana had a point. "Fine. Truce. Shall we?" he asked, pulling himself into the saddle and gesturing for her to do the same.

Diana eased into the saddle with grace. Any concerns he may have had, subsided when she had approached Firefly from the left, talking to the mare with a gentle voice and rubbing her neck to reassure her, letting the horse smell and get acquainted. It bode well for the outing.

"Can I ask you questions as we ride?" Diana asked.

"Ask away," Chad said. Thirty days of questions and answers wasn't much to look forward to, but when they came from the pretty lady buying the farm, he was inclined to overlook the tedious chore.

"Why are you selling? This is such a beautiful property and I haven't seen much past this pasture."

Talk about jumping right into the deep water. He hadn't expected personal questions and wasn't sure he liked the idea. There was only so much he was willing to discuss. "It's a dairy farm. Milk prices bottomed out and everything went into slow decline for a lot of farms. I'm lucky to have been able to hold on this long." And he might have made it if he'd had the support of the community, but that hadn't happened in ten years. Not since his father had robbed the bank at gunpoint, accidentally killing the sheriff, and terrorized many others from the community.

"Paul said something about you having to sell the milk in the next county over in some neighboring towns. Why is that? Seems to me it would be cheaper to stay local."

Paul has a big mouth. "It would be, but there's bad blood between the people in town and me. End of story." It was enough of the truth for Diana to understand his reasoning without all the gory details about his father destroying the lives of his children and others in town. The sheriff had been a good man, and his six kids and wife had been devastated. The healing never came, not that Chad expected it to be different. He understood harboring anger and animosity, something he'd felt toward his dad since that fateful day.

"I'm sorry. Families can be difficult." Diana spoke with a greater understanding than he would have expected and surprised him by not asking for details.

Almost as though she had a story of her own. "This is known as the pond pasture. This is some of the best pasture land for the cows to graze because of the natural water source, the ease of access, and the shade elements. The back forty is another area that I'll show you another time. It's got the Trinity River running through it, making these two the best of the best on the land. It's important the cows have a comfortable grazing area and not be stressed, or it reduces their milk production. It's a little farther from the barn, but I think well worth the benefits."

"Sounds like people have a lot in common with the cows. Okay, so not exactly, not the milk part." She laughed. "I meant the needing a place to stay that gives one the freedom to relax, a place to destress. You asked why I would want the farm…and for me…that's what I'm hoping to get from living here. A place of peace."

Chad shook his head. "You've got it all wrong. Dairy farming is not the cure for stress. It's a lot of work. Regular, monotonous work." They kept riding, the horses sensing where they were and almost on automatic.

"That remains to be seen. Perhaps it's all in the way you look at it. If you love the land, it's a labor of love. That's what my grandmother always used to say." Her eyes clouded over, turning them almost a hazy steel blue.

"Used to say?" he asked.

Firefly did a headshake, almost as if she could sense Diana's change in emotion.

"She died a couple of years ago. I miss her terribly. I didn't get to see her much after I turned ten and my folks had other ideas for my summer vacations, but we talked often. I got to see her more after I turned eighteen on my college breaks. The stories that woman could tell," Diana added, her voice soft with remembrance.

His own grandmother had been the same way. Sweet, loving, and full of wisdom. And he understood the missing part. His mother died while giving birth to his sister, and his grandmother had stepped in to help. At least she had until his father saw fit to move her on. "I'm sure she was a wonderful woman, and it sounds like she knew what she was talking about." It was the same thing Chad knew and understood, and exactly why he was selling the farm and moving to the city. Everything he did here was not, by any stretch of the imagination, a labor of love. He loved certain aspects of the farm, but as a whole, it stood for a part of him he wished to forget. His family past.

They kept riding, Chad answering questions along the way. Arriving at the second pasture, he pointed out the herd to Diana. It wasn't long before the cattle headed his way, some moseying, some running, if it could be called such. Funny, without a doubt.

"*Ummm*, why are they suddenly headed our way? Will they stop before running us over and we become flat as pancakes?"

"It's milking time, and therefore feeding time. This is part of the job you signed on for. You okay helping me herd them back to the milking barn?" An extra pair of hands would be appreciated, especially if Diana had any natural inclination in the herding technique. Something Tonia never had, nor was she willing to learn.

"Sure, but what do I do?" Diana asked, glancing back at the herd nervously.

"You can lead them, although most know the way. Some of the younger calves need guidance. I'll ride in the back to make sure none get left behind or try to wander off. There's a free stall pen area outside the barn and I put them there until we can lead them into the milking stalls. They're sociable creatures and it helps them relax."

"Sounds easy enough." Diana nodded, although the tone of her voice sent a completely different impression.

Leading was the simple part. It was the strays that needed more focus, something he'd let Diana take control of in the coming days. Easing her in was a far better approach if he didn't want her to head for the hills. *Literally.*

Chad used the opportunity to see Diana without her being aware. She was a natural in the saddle. Back straight, long blonde tendrils bouncing cross her back as she went, it was oddly peaceful watching her. All the cows minded their manners, none daring to stray. Perhaps it was the effect of the beautiful lady escorting them to the barn.

He herded small groups of cattle into the barn into the free stall where they could move around until they were moved into position for milking. "I've already put out their feed in the troughs. They get milked twice a day with plenty of fresh food immediately after and then a rest period back out in the pasture for five to six hours." There was so much she had to learn. He couldn't help but once again think this wouldn't end well.

Diana watched how he moved the cows for the first few times and soon joined in, making short order of the process. "So about the milking thing. Do you have the electronic milkers or whatever those things were called again?" she asked, looking back and forth between him and the cows, a frown on her face.

It was as though she suddenly realized what came next if he didn't have an Automatic Milking System. "Well, yes and no," he answered, taking a scene from Diana's own playbook.

"Wise guy. Let's have it."

"I have an **AMS**. It's the commercial system originally installed and can handle up to twenty-six cows at once, in which I ran four milking rounds back when I had a hundred head of cattle. Morning and night. Seven days a week. Broken lines and parts have me down a max of sixteen cows at a time, and then sometimes even that can't be relied on. The system is old and needs updating. I have the electronic milkers. Unfortunately, most need repairs. So the ones that are working, we hooked up to the cows' teats, and well for the rest, we hand milk them the good old-fashioned way. Something every farmer should know how to do."

"I see," she said, looking doubtfully at the oversized Holstein needing her help. "I noticed the repairs needed with the barn doors and the paddock gate. And the roof. And now you mention the milking machines. I'm sorry things got so difficult. Perhaps we could work on some repairs together."

Talking about the repairs was a stall tactic, but one he didn't particularly care for. "Repairs cost money. It's not just the labor." A man had his pride and talking about money, or the lack thereof, never sat well.

Diana moved to stand closer. "You know, since I'm buying the place, I could pay for them."

"No." His flat refusal came out a little rough around the edges, but it ran all over him in a way he hadn't expected. Yes, she was buying the place, but until the deal closed, it was still his farm. And he'd do things his way.

"Well, okay then," Diana said, clearly not in agreement, but willing to concede.

"Quit stalling, and I'll show you how to milk a cow. Then you can try it, because if you want to keep what's left of the herd, you need to know how to do the milking with no problem. A cow that's not milked regularly causes them pain, something any decent dairy farmer should avoid." Chad grabbed the milking bucket and stool and sat down next to the first cow.

"I learned that much in college," Diana quipped, shooting him a "be real" glance.

"Oh?" he said, unable to contain his surprise. Assuming she meant vet school, it begged an answer about why she wasn't a vet now? "What did you study?" he asked, trying to understand her better.

"Animal science. Large animal science," she clarified.

"Well, that would have been something you could have mentioned previously."

"I could have, but it didn't occur to me you'd want to know. Besides, I feel there's a world of difference between text book milking and the real thing." She shot him a grin and then glanced down at her watch. "Oh no, I hate to watch you milk and run, but I've got to go pick Lindsey up from school." Diana was halfway to the barn door before he could stand.

"What about the milking? You need to learn how to do this," he called out after her.

"Tomorrow. There's always tomorrow."

Twenty-nine tomorrows and counting. Chad shook his head and settled back into the chore of milking by himself, just like he'd done for umpteen years. The woman wouldn't learn a thing if she didn't apply herself, but it would be her problem at the end of the month. Except, the idea of the farm falling completely apart didn't sit well. True, it needed some fixing up, but the place wasn't beyond repair.

A part of him had hoped the new owner would bring it back to life. Bring it back to the way it once was when he was a child and had first arrived. The excitement and wonder he'd felt had long since been buried with his father, but it didn't mean he wanted the place to fail.

Chapter Six

♥

Lindsey's trepidation about going to school this morning was very different from yesterday. A couple of new friends and an amazing first-grade teacher had a way of making everything right. Now if only Diana's own trepidation would ease up enough to unfurl the gripping tension centered in the pit of her stomach.

Last night's research on milking cows gave her plenty of refresher information from what she'd learned in college, but the actual hands on...well, that would happen today. And no video would come close to the real thing. It was daunting to think of how much control you thought you had when doing the chore but do it wrong and the cow would let you know who was boss. And there were plenty of videos online to prove it, although she saw nothing funny in watching someone get kicked.

Diana crossed town, turning onto the long driveway that led to the Thompson place. Soon to become the Langley farm. Langley's Lonestar Farm had a nice ring to it. As she exited the car, Chad appeared as if by magic from the direction of the barn. He either had ears like a hawk or he'd been watching for her. More than likely the first, unless it was because he was still hoping she wouldn't be back for round two. He'd said as much yesterday.

"Good morning," she called out.

"Morning," he said with a tip of his hat before glancing down at his watch. "Much better arrival time, although, when you're on your own, the day will need to start at sunup if you plan to get all the work done by sundown."

Diana frowned. "All work and no play...well, you know the saying. I can always hire someone to help me if needed. I don't see myself going it alone, and Lindsey needs me more than the farm."

"If you say so." Chad shook his head. "A dairy farm needs to be profitable for hired help, something that hasn't happened in a long time around here. Place has been more like a slow bleed on aspirin."

Mr. Negative was in rare form this morning. "Fresh ideas might just change all that."

"Perhaps." Chad shrugged. "After you," he gestured toward the barn. "I thought we'd start with cows. I've already finished most of the morning round of milking, but I saved a few just for you since you ran out on the chore yesterday. Need to make sure you know what to do and then you'll have lots of time to practice the rest of the month."

His smirk had *her wondering exactly what a* few meant. "I'm all yours. Three or thirty, I'm up for the challenge." As long as they didn't kick her.

"We'll see about that, Miss Sunshine."

Diana shot him a grin. "That's a lovely thing to say. Thank you." She knew he didn't mean it as a compliment, but she couldn't help but take the words to heart in a positive way. God had led her to this place, and if her attitude had sunshine in it, then all the better. It was something she hadn't felt in a long time, and she intended to take hold and not let go. This was their new life and she would do everything in her power to turn the place into a successful dairy farm, for Lindsey's sake.

The barn door creaked as he pulled it open, the potent aroma of manure causing her to scrunch her face in distaste.

Chad chuckled.

The softer lines of his expression were at her expense but considering how much more approachable they made the man, it was well worth it. "I spent some time refreshing my memory about the process last night, but can you show me what to do? Somehow, the cows seem bigger in person."

"And stronger smelling," he teased, his grin widening.

"That too," she agreed, appreciating his sense of humor.

He led her to the cow, grabbed a milk can from the shelf nearby, and pulled up a stool. "First, let her know you're here. A hand on her back. A few kind words. Less tension in the cow produces more milk as she lets go." Chad demonstrated by running a hand across the cow's back. "Good girl, Sadie May. Time for milking and we've got a newbie to show how it's done."

It was pretty much what she'd learned from the videos, but somehow, this seemed more person-able. Real. "Talking to a cow. I never would have guessed."

Chad looked up at her but quickly returned to the task at hand.

Diana's solution was to fix the machines, but he was right. She needed to not only know how, but to be comfortable. "Fine. Show me how, boss." She enjoyed teasing him. The cowboy's smile was most rewarding when he loosened up a bit.

"Gently pull down on her teats one at a time until she lets go and the milk flows. Then keep milking and tugging until she's finished. That's it. Oh, and stay out from behind her when you're done. Otherwise, a good swift kick might cost you a can of milk and a dousing you won't forget." He talked through the process without so much as a peek in her direction, staying focused on the task at hand.

"Did you learn that lesson the hard way?" she asked.

"I did. When I was twelve." Chad shot her a wink as the milk squirted into the can. He stood. "Your turn now that she's primed. You can milk Sadie Mae, and then there are four others I left for you. Once you get the hang of it, I'll get started on mucking the stalls and you can help finish. If we both hurry and finish up in here, I thought we could ride out, and I'd show you the other side of the property."

"*Ummm*, okay." The tension between her shoulder blades increased, and she rolled her head to loosen up. Diana wanted to tackle this process like a pro, needing a few wins in the challenge column to help rebuild her confidence. Confidence Silas had taken from her...but not anymore. That part of her life was over.

She patted the cow's back, imitating Chad. "Good girl. I promise to be more gentle than the last guy. Men don't understand."

Sadie Mae swung her head back. "*Mooooo*," she bellowed, causing Diana to jump.

Chad laughed. "She likes you. Keep going." He moved to stand next to Diana.

She sat on the stool and reached for a teat. It felt leathery in her hand, but warm. Life flowing energy filled the palms of her hands as she squeezed and pulled. Except nothing came out. She glanced up at Chad, not sure of what she was doing wrong.

"Gentle but determined. It's not like squeezing a tube of toothpaste," he teased. Sadie Mae mooed a second time. "And I reckon she'd like to get on with the milking. She feels better afterward."

Diana shook her head, not sure how more *determined* would make the cow feel better.

Chad leaned over Diana, taking her hands in his and molding them around two teats. Clenching her fingers tighter, they pulled, milk shooting into the can.

"I get it. Thanks." Diana remained focused on the cow, unwilling to let Chad see the flush of her cheeks. The man had a way of getting under her skin with his nearness, not that she would let him know. Surely it was a simple case of cowboy appreciation because anything else, she wasn't interested.

Chad stepped back and Diana tried again, this time doing it on her own. It was a proud moment, and she peered up at Chad, pleased to see his look of approval. A look that quickly turned to laughter.

"Look at what you're doing and not me. Aim is better."

She turned back to the task at hand, only to see the last few squirts had missed the milk can entirely. Her faced flushed with heat yet again, for an entirely different reason. Embarrassment. She forced herself to continue, staying focused so as not to make the same mistake twice. That was a personal rule of hers. Never make the same mistake twice. Which is why she'd sworn off men and relationships and that applied doubly so to a good-looking cowboy who could make her laugh.

When the milk stopped flowing, Diana sat up straight, rolling her shoulders back to stretch her neck. She flexed her fingers and rubbed them, easing the ache. Milking a cow was a lot more work than she planned. Luckily, they had machines to do the process, as milking fifty cows would never be something she could handle. Especially not multiple times a day. And then, to be profitable, the herd had to be expanded.

Four more cows and an aching back later, she stood, satisfied with her efforts. "Done," she called out, looking around for Chad.

He came out of one of the nearby stalls. "Great. Slow, but good job for your first time. Or maybe you planned it that way to get out of helping me muck the stalls."

Diana grinned. She hadn't planned it that way but talk about a bonus. "Not me."

"When do you need to pick up Lindsey?" he asked.

"One-thirty today. It's a teacher workday. Why?"

"Then how about we just take a quick ride out and we can check the cows? Then we can be back here in time for you to pick her up. Then, if it's okay with you, we can all ride out together when I show you the rest of the property."

She raised an eyebrow, surprised by his suggestion. Lindsey would be over the moon if she knew, but there was no way Diana could say yes. "I'm not sure I'm good enough on a horse to take Lindsey with me, and she certainly doesn't know how to ride alone."

"I realize that, but it's not like she can't ride with me. I used to take my younger sister out all the time and we rode double. It was a great way for her to learn the feel of a horse and subtle cues that happen between a horse and rider. Of course, it was also a great way to keep an eye on her." Chad chuckled.

"So you were the unhappy brother tasked with babysitting her?"

"No. I was the eighteen-year-old brother all too happy to take over raising my eight-year-old sister when the need struck."

His comment only stirred up more questions. Life must have been very difficult for him and her heart ached for the young boy who suddenly had the responsibility of a sister and a farm. "I see. I heard she just got married."

"She did. Which is why I find myself in the position of being able to sell the ranch and move on. Her husband is a good guy and she won't need me anymore."

"I see. So the wedding dress—"

"Is hers. Married right here at the farm."

It explained a lot about his situation. "Oh, at first I thought perhaps you had just gotten married and your new wife wasn't keen on ranch living."

His calm manner vanished in the blink of an eye. "You thought wrong. I had a girlfriend who moved to the city, and she left with another guy. Turns out neither one of us was cut out for country living."

"Or maybe she was the wrong woman," Diana said in a low voice, touching his arm.

Chad's gaze drifted to her hand, his brow furrowed with deep lines. "Wrong woman. Wrong place. All the same. Marriage doesn't appeal to me, which was part of the problem with Tonia."

Diana nodded. "See, we have something in common. Marriage doesn't appeal to me either."

"But I take it you were married, *ummm*...seeing as Lindsey...*ummm*..."

"I was. Lindsey's father isn't a nice guy and we are better off without him." They'd crossed into a territory Diana preferred to avoid, but she could tell how difficult it had been for him to form the question. "Trusting someone else isn't a mistake I will make again. Not with Lindsey as part of the equation. She deserves happiness and I aim to make sure she gets it."

Chad looked relieved he hadn't stepped into a pile of manure with his comment. "Yeah, you come across as a devoted mom."

"Thank you. I am trying. And with God to guide me, I'm sure it will all work out. He led me here, after all." Diana believed it with all her heart.

Chad frowned. "I think it's more a case of you turned down a road with a rumbling stomach and a plan to picnic where you didn't belong," he teased.

"That's where you're wrong. Turns out, I do belong." Diana shot him a smile as he finished checking the horses' saddles.

"Shall we?" he asked, clicking his heels to his horse's flanks gently to lead the way, effectively putting an end to the conversation.

Diana followed him across the field, loving the freedom of riding again. Moving together as one, her rhythm quickly fell into sync as they picked up speed into a canter.

It was a good ten minutes before Chad slowed. He pointed off in the distance. "That's Ruffian. The last bull on the ranch."

"But what about the other bull, where Lindsey and me were going to picnic?" she asked, frowning at him. Surely this isn't the same place. If it was, Diana was all turned around.

Chad grinned. "*Ummm*...this is the bull, and you were never in danger. But you could have been, is the point," he added.

Diana tensed. "You lied." There had been enough of that with Silas to last a lifetime.

"Not really. I was making a point. Ruffian is real and he can get out, which is why checking his fences regularly is extremely important," he said, defending his actions.

"*Hmmpphh.* Stretch of the truth, perhaps, but your point is well taken." Diana couldn't help but remember the fear that lodged in the pit of her stomach when Chad had mentioned the bull. Fear for Lindsey. But now, as they approached, she couldn't help but admire the hulking beast in all his glory. "So, why do you still have him?"

"You can't impregnate cows without a bull. It would have been the final death knoll to the dairy farm."

"I see. So you weren't ready to give up completely?"

Chad frowned. "I guess not, but that's a moot point now. The place is sold, and he's all yours."

His words landed with finality, and the dawning truth struck her hard. This would be her dairy farm soon, and everything, including responsibility for the place, would fall on her shoulders. It was an overwhelming thought, but the trickle of excitement had started and she hoped with each passing day, her love for the place would become like a river of love.

Chapter Seven

♥

As much as Chad didn't like being roped into playing the role of mentor for the month, there was no denying his student was attractive. Not to mention downright entertaining. He'd noticed the cute way her eyebrow twitched when she was concentrating on milking the cow, the effect enough to make him chuckle. Not that he said anything to her, the moment too memorable to ruin.

After throwing a few snacks and waters in a saddlebag, Chad waited on the porch for Diana to return with Lindsey. Glancing around the ranch, he saw it through the eyes of a newcomer. Chipped and peeling white paint on the house and barn. Fences sadly in need of staining. A hole in the barn roof he still hadn't fixed. Everywhere he looked, he saw loads of repairs that needed to be done.

Why Diana wanted to buy the place, he couldn't fathom. Even the front steps could use a few boards replaced. And it wasn't that he hadn't worked from sunup to sundown to make it all work. His efforts were just never enough. Not for the farm or Tonia. It was as though the two had competed for his time and attention, and only Chad had come out on the losing end.

A blue car appeared as it headed for the house, dust swirling in its wake. Chad stepped off the porch and smiled as Lindsey bound out of the car, her face wreathed in a smile.

"Is it true?" she asked, running up to him, her blue eyes wide as saucers.

"Is what true?" Chad asked, fairly certain what the little girl meant, but enjoying her moment of excitement.

"That we're going horseback riding and I get to ride shotgun with you?"

Chad chuckled. "Yes. But where on earth did you hear the term shotgun?"

"Mommy. She said I was going to ride shotgun with you. When I asked what it meant, she said, in front of you. You have a really big horse, but I won't be afraid. Not with you keeping me safe," Lindsey said, bestowing him with a confidence he didn't feel he had earned.

It was daunting. "It's known as riding double, and usually not something done. But since you're small and haven't ridden before, I thought you'd enjoy getting to know what it feels like to ride a horse. Duchess is well-trained and I totally trust her ability for the two of us to ride safely together." The times he rode together with his sister were actually some of the best memories. And now, Lindsey's trust and faith in him were awe-inspiring.

"Woohoo. I want to learn to ride, but Mommy says I have to wait until we get me a kid-size horse."

"That's a good idea, but there are some things we can do in the meantime to speed up the process," he said, shooting her a wink. It had been fourteen years since he had introduced his sister to riding, but she still loved it and, in fact, was quite good. Roxanne had learned the basic fundamentals from him, but it was her drive to excel on her own that led to her success in junior barrel-racing competitions. It had been a proud moment for Chad, reinforcing his role as a parent ever since his father was incarcerated.

Technically, he'd been parenting his sister from the minute she came home from the hospital as a baby and motherless. Chad had been ten at the time and his father hadn't done much in the way of parenting. It was almost as if his father resented Roxanne for what could never be termed her fault. No one could have known about his mother's aneurysm, and the strain of childbirth only hastened what would have happened soon anyway.

"Ready to go?" he asked as Diana stepped up on the porch, sliding her phone in a back pocket.

"Sure thing. My friend from back home needed some information, and I wanted to take care of it before we set out. Now my phone's on mute and I'm all yours," she said, warming him with her sweet smile.

"Perfect." They walked to the barn where the horses were tied to a rail, saddled and ready to ride. He untied the reins of Firefly and held them out to Diana.

"Thank you. Do you want me to hand Lindsey up to you first before I mount? It might make it easier,' Diana offered.

"Sure thing." Chad took Duchess's reins in hand and slid into the saddle. He leaned forward to help hoist Lindsey up as Diana lifted her. He settled her in front of him, keeping both arms around her to prevent Lindsey from sliding off. "Hold on to the saddle horn. It will help you stay more stable and feel more secure."

"Got it. This is really high up here. I won't fall, will I?" she asked, a slight quiver to her voice.

It was a healthy fear as far as Chad was concerned. One had to respect the power of a horse and its massive size. "You'll be just fine. Relax and enjoy the ride. I'll try to explain some things as we go."

Diana saddled up, and they headed out, taking the path to cut to the back forty. His favorite place on the ranch.

"Is everything okay? With your friend, I mean," Chad asked, more than a little curious about Diana and her sudden appearance in town and desire to buy a farm unexpectedly.

"Yes, Allison is taking care of a school record I need for Pineview Elementary."

"I like Miss Allison. She's the best. And that's where I got my middle name. Lindsey Allison Gibson," Lindsey announced proudly.

"I thought your last name was Langley?" Chad asked, directing the question at Diana.

"It is," Lindsey answered before her mother had a chance. "Gibson is my daddy's last name, but him and mommy got divorced. So now I'm a Langley."

Diana swung around to look at her daughter, the pronouncement clearly catching her by surprise. She remained out of the discussion, instead turning her focus back to Firefly and the trail ahead of them.

Chad was tempted to ask Diana to explain, but perhaps that was for a later discussion, when her daughter wasn't around. "Just relax," he explained to Lindsey, noticing how stiff she was holding herself. "I want you to feel how the horse moves. Watch the signals I give whether by reins or voice."

"Gotcha." Lindsey beamed up at him. "Look, Mommy. I'm riding on a really big horse," she called out.

Diana slowed and came alongside of them. "You sure are. Promise me you'll listen to Chad," she said, giving Lindsey the mother-daughter stare.

It was the same intense look he used to use on Roxanne when he wanted her to pay close attention. "Let's ride out to the southern border first. It's the nicest part of the property. And judging by your choice of picnic location, it will rank high on your list of favorites."

"Let me guess...more bluebonnets?" Diana asked, grinning at him.

Chad nodded. "More than you can imagine. It's closer to the mountains and slightly cooler. More than perfect for the Texas wildflower. "Like a special magical place." It's what he used to tell Roxanne.

"I think they're so pretty. Can I pick some of your flowers to take back with me?" Lindsey asked.

"Of course. They're almost yours now anyway, and I reckon you can pick them every day if you want to. At least while they are in season."

"Do you hear that, Mommy? I can pick them whenever I want. Let's go," she said, eager to see this special place.

Chad and Lindsey led the way, the little girl commenting on everything she saw. A non-stop chatterbox. But with her holding up most of the conversation, it gave Chad the opportunity to take in the sights. He couldn't remember the last time he'd ridden out this way on a pleasure ride, and some sights caught him off guard.

The old oak tree off to the left in the distance. The one where he built a fort. And the one he fell out of and broke his arm. His father claimed he'd done it on purpose to get out of work. The truth was worse. He'd fallen because he was showing off for a girl. Talk about humiliation.

"Let's head to the right. The Trinity River runs through the property here and it's one of the best pastures, one that doesn't need water pumped in to feed the cattle."

"*Hmmm*, so the other pastures have water pumps to fill the water troughs?"

"Yes, except for the section with the pond. And unless we're in a drought, that stays fairly full. And when the pumps to the other pastures break, it's extremely expensive to fix them, so keep up on the maintenance. Far cry better than a repair bill."

Diana nodded. "I'll keep that in mind."

"Also, this is the prime piece of land, and not one you should lease out. But the others, until you get more cows, or should I say, if, then consider leasing out the pastures. You are paying a hefty price for the farm, and if you don't want to lose the place to the bank, it's a good option."

"Leasing? People rent land? For what?" she asked.

"For the hay. Or pasture for horses, sheep, or cattle, mainly. It's what I would have done next if I hadn't sold the property. I put it off as long as I could." The idea of strangers from town using his property never sat well. It would have been different if he had felt like a part of the community. But he didn't, so he had kept it as his very last choice to stay afloat.

Diana shook her head. "I don't think I'll be leasing my land. The solitude of the place is part of the appeal."

It was exactly the same thing he'd thought, but ideas didn't pay bills. "Suit yourself." He could offer suggestions, but what she did with the place was entirely up to her. This time next month, his biggest concern would be what entertainment venue or restaurant he wanted to visit, the prospect more than appealing.

"This place is beautiful. I've never seen so many wild flowers. What's that?" Diana asked, pointing to the tree in the distance.

It was obvious she had spotted the wooden structure built into the branches. "That's an old fort I built when I was a kid. Great place to get away from the drudgery of farm life. It hasn't been used in years."

They rode toward the tree, stopping beneath it as they gazed up at the fort. It seemed so much smaller now. "You should have it checked out if you plan on letting Lindsey use it." It was his special place and not one he shared with others, but Diana didn't need that little tidbit of information.

"For sure."

"I have a fort?" Lindsey exclaimed. "Cool. Wait till I tell the kids at school."

Diana laughed. "Did you play here a lot as a child, then?"

"Chores got in the way more often than not. But when I could sneak off, I came here. If you listen, you can hear the river, and from up there," he said, pointing up to the top of the fort, "you can see the Trinity River where it runs across the farm. The fort was a brilliant spot to hide out and watch the wildlife. Some good fishing down there, too." Being here brought up a wealth of emotions he hadn't expected. Memory lane was best left closed.

Diana shot him a questioning glance. "Sounds to me like you miss coming here. Why is that when you're an adult now and own the place? One would think you could visit any time you wanted."

"Adulthood only brought on more chores and less time. And taking care of my little sister took up any free time I had. Not that I regret those times we shared. She was a handful but kept me on my toes." But being here now, he regretted not making time to visit his childhood fort, if just for the solitude and peace it always brought him.

"Well, maybe you should come back out here alone, just to relive the memory. I hate the thought of you leaving without taking the time to enjoy such a special place that obviously means something to you."

"I don't know. Maybe." Chad reined in Duchess at the river and helped Lindsey off the horse, using one arm wrapped around her waist to lower her to the ground. He glanced around and sucked in a deep breath, inhaling the smell of the river and trees, topped with a healthy dose of bluebonnet fragrance. It reminded him of the good side of the past, a side he'd long since forgotten.

"Can I play in the water?" Lindsey asked, taking a few steps closer to the river.

Diana shook her head. "Not this time, sweetie. Chad's going to finish showing us around."

Chad slid out of the saddle. "I brought some snacks and water. Might be a good place for a break," he offered.

"That was thoughtful of you." Diana turned back to Lindsey. "You can play for a bit, but don't get wet."

"Deal," Lindsey said, taking off and running through the field. "Mommy, look at the pretty butterflies," she called out, her hands held high as if trying to catch one.

"Thank you for this. It means a lot to me to get to see the land through your eyes. At least the good parts," she added.

"You're welcome. I just hope you're up for the not-so-good parts." At least half a foot shorter than him, her well-toned arms didn't shout muscular, and therefore Chad wasn't sure she was up to the task.

But then, as a boy, it's not like he hadn't grown into the job.

Maybe for Diana, it would be the same.

Chapter Eight

♥

Every muscle in Diana's body ached. Hot baths after she had put Lindsey to bed, did little to ease the weariness or the overwhelming sense that buying the farm might have been a mistake. What started out as doubts had grown into a full-blown panic that wouldn't go away. It was a lot of work for Chad, how on earth did she think she could manage it on her own?

The problem was, she'd come too far to walk away. Lindsey loved it here and was settling in at school. She had promised her daughter they would stay and so they would. The daily routine was the same. Drop Lindsey off at school.

Head to the ranch for more tutorials about the ins and outs of a dairy farm. Pick Lindsey up and head back to the farm for more lessons. Although the afternoon was a lighter schedule so they could keep an eye on her daughter.

Today Chad promised her a trip to Wylie and Fontana, where he would introduce her to his buyers. Something she'd been meaning to ask him about, and now she would get her chance. It also sounded way more fun than mucking stalls, which was just one of the daily chores she was slowly getting used to. The scent of manure, urine, and sweat was overpowering, and it clung to her clothes like a second skin. Perhaps in time, loving the land and all that came with the farm would override the negative aspect of that particular chore.

Diana pulled into the driveway. Chad stood talking to the driver of the milk tanker. It was already loaded and ready to go. That part of her education on dairy farming was easy, more so because it was by the book. X hours, x temperature, and all quality tested to fill the dairy farm motto...*Keep it clean. Keep it cold. Keep it moving.* It was a detailed process that ensured fresh milk was delivered to the processing center daily in order that the milk could be packaged on a grocery store shelf within days. Farm fresh.

She herself had milked some of those cows whose milk would end up on someone's table. It was an awe-inspiring thought, one that hit her with a sense of peace. A job well done and her efforts would not be going to waste. A novel concept and one completely opposite of the way things had been under her parent's roof and then living with Silas.

Refusing to go down memory lane, she shoved open the door, exited the car, and headed in Chad's direction. "Good morning," she called out, waving in his direction.

Chad tipped his hat in her direction. "Morning,"

His deep gravelly voice was comforting, the knowledge he was still here and would be for the rest of the month, calming her earlier qualms. "What's with the trailer?" she asked, noticing his Chevy and the long black trailer hitched to it.

"There's an old tractor I'm delivering to a guy in Fontana. Thought we'd knock out the delivery while you met the processors I sell the milk to."

"Sounds like a plan. I'd love to meet more people in the area. Connections if you will." Late night research turned up several good ideas for saving the farm...ideas that required money. Money she had. Connections she didn't. Not to mention, help was on the short list, but she'd known that going into this crazy plan of hers to become a dairy farmer.

"You know, you're going to need a truck to pull the cattle trailer and haul stuff around."

"Oh, dear. I hadn't thought of that." Diana frowned. Spending more money wasn't the issue, bringing attention to her financial status...that was a problem. "Any interest in selling me your truck? Or, if not, do you have any suggestions of where I might find something used?"

"Sorry, my truck isn't part of the bargain. I've had Betsy for almost twenty years and she runs like a dream."

Diana cocked one eyebrow up, shocked at his comment and what it revealed. "Betsy, huh? Didn't take you for a name-your-truck kind of guy."

"What kind of guy is that?" he asked, his forehead drawn tight.

"You know, like the friendly cowboy kind," she said, truly interested. People usually named their children, horses, and pets with some level of attachment or reasoning, which made her curious about how he came up with Betsy.

"And I'm not friendly?" he asked, not bothering to explain.

"I didn't say that. Never mind," she said, shaking her head. It was a losing battle to explain what she meant, especially given she wasn't sure herself, and given the man was like a closed book. Glimpses here and there, but never enough to get a good read.

"Fair enough. As to where to buy a truck, Channel Motors down on Main Street is a decent place. Victor will give you a good deal and is as honest as they come."

"Thanks, I'll check it out. I'm glad you pointed out the shortfall." It was times like this that made her waiver in her decision, and some of her earlier insecurities settled back in place. How could she not have thought about something as simple as needing a vehicle to handle the job on the farm?

Chad pulled open the passenger door. "Let's roll."

"Thank you. Maybe you are the friendly cowboy type, after all." She grinned and pulled the door shut. The temptation to ask was strong. What's the worst he could do...say *mind your own business*? "So where's the name Betsy from?" she asked when he slid in behind the steering wheel.

"It was my grandmother's name."

Diana was in shock he'd answered the question, more so because of the answer. "And sentimental to boot. My heart be still." Diana shook her head, finding herself liking her new friend way more than she should and not necessarily for his well-toned muscular strength.

"Don't tell anyone. They wouldn't believe you anyway," Chad retorted.

"Then why don't you tell me about your grandmother? Seems we were both lucky to have a special grandparent in our lives."

Chad frowned, and for the space of a few seconds remained silent. It was as though he were considering her question, or even whether to answer. He let out a deep breath. "I credit her with my ability to step in and take care of my sister when things got rough. She tried to help as much as possible, but my dad and her didn't agree on much of anything when it came to Roxanne. When she died, she left me the truck. I keep it running smoothly, just like she always did. It's my way of honoring her."

If Diana hadn't been looking Chad's way, she would have missed the tightening of his jaw. A dead giveaway there was more to the story than he was letting on. "So, where are we headed first? She asked, more than ready to press for more information.

"Wylie."

Short and to the point. Diana jumped right in and ignored his subtle clues that he didn't like to talk about himself or the past. "I know this isn't your favorite subject, but why don't you sell locally? Seems to me it would be cheaper for the processors and therefore more profit for you from increased sales. *Bad blood* doesn't explain much." It was the term he'd used before dropping the subject and leaving her hanging with basically no real information.

Another glance, this one accompanied by a shake of his head. "It would make things more profitable. The problem is the buyers at the plant in town don't want Thompson farm milk. End of story." Chad's focus remained on the road this time.

"But why? Can't you explain to me what's going on? I deserve to know since I'm buying the farm, don't you think?" Whatever it was had to be huge, because to hear Chad tell it...it was almost as if the town had ostracized him. She couldn't imagine anything he would have done that would call for that type of treatment.

"*Hmmpphh.* Stick around town long enough and you'll find out."

"Please," she said, dropping her voice a notch and laying her hand on his arm.

His gaze flicked down to where her hand lay and then up at her. "Suffice to say there's no reason *you* can't sell here locally. It's me they hate...or should I say, my father, and me by extension."

"But if it's your father..."

"Sins of the father are laid at the feet of his children. Something my sister and I know all too well," he ground out, anger echoing in each word. "Enough of that subject. I'll introduce you to my current buyers, but what you do after that is up to you."

"Just one more question. Will this issue of yours with the town affect me living here and becoming a part of the community? Will it affect Lindsey?"

"Nope. The only way you would become involved is if you made the mistake of falling in love with me," he said, suddenly flashing her a wide grin as he put the truck in park and jumped out of the vehicle.

Not that running away would get him off the hook. "Good. Because we *both* know there's zero chance of that happening. But don't think this subject is closed just because you say so." She lifted her chin in defiance and followed him into the building at their first stop.

"Yes, it is."

Hours later, Chad got them back to the farm, Diana having just enough time to head to Pineview Elementary to pick up Lindsey without being added to the officially-late list. Meeting and talking with the buyers had taken longer than expected, everyone curious about her intentions with the farm. It was a valid concern knowing supply and demand played a big part in their business. She wasn't ready to reveal the plans she'd been working on. That would come in time after everything else was settled. Life was complicated enough at the moment without adding to it.

"Did you have a good day at school, honey?" Diana asked as she helped Lindsey slide into the back seat and locking her seatbelt in place.

"I did. I made a new friend. Her name is Maddie, and she has a horse. Can we get my horse now that we are going to live on a farm? Lots of kids here have horses. Can I please, Mommy?"

"Not yet, sweetheart. We don't own the place yet, but once we get settled in, I'll look into it. Patience is always good." Glancing in the rearview mirror, she couldn't help but notice Lindsey's frown. Lately there had been a lot more high notes than low, but a kid not getting their way would always be a low. Her daughter didn't understand, but then, she shouldn't have to.

She'd been through so much lately and had been a trooper through most of it. Most little girls wouldn't understand why their father didn't want to be a part of their life, but somehow she'd reasoned it all out in her head. Not that Diana hadn't considered it was all an act...something she was determined to keep an eye on.

Lindsey was quiet the rest of the way to the farm, leaving Diana time to think through some of the other issues that needed attending. Her things-to-do-before-Chad-left list was growing instead of lessening like it should, adding more stress to her already full plate.

The second Diana switched off the engine, Lindsey hopped out of the car and started running toward the barn. Chad was headed in their direction, so it was easy to allow her daughter the freedom to run, hoping it would restore her good mood. A new friend was a big deal and Diana would need to remember to ask more about the girl at dinner.

Lindsey was back in a flash, her eyes wide with excitement. Gone was the sullen child of moments ago.

"Can I, Mommy? Can I?"

Chad joined them, a mischievous grin on his face. Whatever the man was up to, clearly had Lindsey in a tizzy.

"Can you what?" Diana asked, glancing up at Chad for information.

"Ride a horse. Not my own, cause you said I couldn't have one yet...but Chad said he got a horse just my size. Didn't you, Chad?" She pulled on his arm eagerly. "Tell her."

Chad nodded before pulling off his cowboy hat. He swiped at his forehead and replaced his Stetson. "I do, but it's not what you're thinking, Diana. I offered to give Lindsey a lesson, one that amounts to me leading her around the ring. Something akin to a pony ride, if you will. I talked to a guy in Wylie that I know, and he agreed to deliver the horse."

Diana had missed the interchange, but the result was the same. The man was full of surprises. Chad had been kind to Lindsey, something Silas couldn't do for his own daughter. "Oh, in that case, sure thing. As long as you are right there with her." She trusted Chad completely.

"Great. I figured she was due for some fun, and that this would be a nice reward for patience this past week."

More evidence of Chad's softie heart. "Well, your timing is perfect, as she wasn't too happy. I wouldn't agree to buy her a horse. Seems all the other kids in town have one, or to hear her tell it, they do," she added, knowing children had a propensity to exaggerate.

"Most do around here," Chad said, shooting Diana a wink.

"Yippee...I'm going to ride a horse. Wait till I tell Maddie. Then I'll be like the other kids and maybe they'll all like me."

"Lindsey, honey, listen to me. Friends should be with you based on who you are, not what you have or don't have. Keep that in mind when you choose your friends, as the heart is a better judge of character." It was an over-the-top explanation for a six-year-old, but it was such an important lesson. And one that in Diana's opinion, could never be started too early.

"Yes, Mommy," Lindsey said, pulling her toward the barn.

Her daughter's easy agreement didn't mean she was taking in every word and engraving them on her heart. More likely, it was a way for her daughter to ride a horse sooner. *The kid way*, as Diana liked to refer to it.

"The pony's name is Dawning Light. I'll saddle her up and meet you at the pen. Deal?" Chad asked.

"Deal," Lindsey chirped, reversing the direction she was headed to lead Diana to the pen.

They walked hand in hand, swinging their arms like best buddies. But then, they were. "You pay attention to what Chad tells you to do, sweetheart. And if you get scared, be sure to speak up. It's okay if you want to stop the ride."

Lindsey scowled. "Like that'll happen. I love horses and Dawning Light just has to love me back." Her daughter climbed on the pen railing and hung on, peering in the direction she expected Chad to appear.

Five minutes later, he led a small horse out of the barn. Lindsey jumped down and ran to Chad's side, reaching out to pet the pony's head, Chad guiding her in the proper method. It wasn't long before he lifted Lindsey up and settled her on the saddle. Diana could hear him giving her instructions, but she couldn't quite make out what was being said. Her daughter beamed in her direction, just as Chad led the pony around the ring.

"Look, Mommy. I'm riding a horse."

"Yes, sweetheart, you are. You look like a natural up there." Diana was so proud of her daughter for being brave enough to try something new. Pulling out her phone, she snapped off several photos, several of them including Chad. She couldn't help but snap a few of just Chad as she noted the expression of peace on his face. He was a natural at working with Lindsey, but then he was experienced with his own sister. But it was the awe and wonder she captured in his expression she found the most intriguing.

Round and round, Chad led Lindsey around on the pony. And the whole time, Lindsey asked questions, her smile never slipping. *Fearless* came to mind.

It had been cloudy all day, but now the sky darkened noticeably. Diana glanced up and frowned. The wind was picking up, the clouds rolling faster across the sky. She checked her phone, only to discover a heavy thunderstorm warning had been issued, one that she missed with her phone on silent and while focused on taking photos. After checking the radar, it was clear this wouldn't be a hit or miss. Pop-up storms came and went, but this one popped up and appeared to be settling in.

"Chad," she called out. "There's a wicked storm rolling in. The weather app says rain in twenty-two minutes."

He led the pony in Diana's direction. "Those things are always wrong, but we should get Dawning Light back into the barn, just in case." Moving toward Lindsey, he reached up and plucked her from the saddle, setting her on the ground.

"*Awww*, shucks. I was having fun." Lindsey said, pouting.

"We'll do this again, don't worry. You did great," Chad reassured her as they passed nearby and headed through the gate.

"Yay. I can't wait." Lindsey took Chad's free hand and walked with him.

Diana followed close behind, unable to stop herself from admiring Chad. He was a natural with kids, like he knew what to say and how to say it. Something Silas had never got right.

Chad unsaddled the pony and led her to a stall. "Sounds like it's already started to rain. So much for twenty-two minutes."

"Guess you were right about them being wrong." Diana laughed. "We need to leave in order to get back to the inn before the worst of the storm hits."

A crack of thunder echoed through the barn, the pony shying away to the back of the stall.

They headed for the front exit, Chad pulling open the barn door. Torrential rains poured from the sky, the trees dancing as they whistled in the wind. "Or by the looks of things, it's already too late and you should stay here."

"I don't think that's a good idea. We don't know how long this will last." Diana frowned. Call her old-fashioned, but after Silas she didn't want to be beholden to anyone...for anything, nor did she want to become the subject of idle gossip.

"I'll head over to the bunkhouse if it makes you feel any better. This looks like official Texas tornado weather, something I don't need a weather app to tell me. They roll in unexpected and all you can do is batten down the hatches until it blows over."

Diana shook her head. "I hear you, but we need to leave."

"Suit yourself. Call and let me know when you get to the inn, so I know you're safe."

They ran for the house, getting quite wet. Diana opened the back door of the car for Lindsey and helped her inside. "Bye, and thanks," she called out over the roar of the wind, before starting the car and backing up. She pressed the accelerator down, intent on making quick work of the return trip to town. Seven minutes under normal conditions, ten minutes tops. Janice would also worry about them until they arrived back at Serendipity.

The windshield wipers danced back and forth furiously but did little to improve the view. Watery blur was the color of the moment. A dark massive shape started to fall across the road, almost as if in slow motion. Diana slammed on her brakes to avoid a collision with the monstrous tree as it shook the road, crushing the front of the car under the weight of its branches and leaves.

Lindsey screamed.

Diana wanted to, but no sound came out.

The realization that had they left a second earlier, they would have been crushed was terrifying. *A Texas tornado.* Chad, it would seem, might be right, and Diana shouldn't be out on the road. Not that she had much choice at this point but to turn around and go back, except her car wouldn't be going anywhere. Not now, maybe never, judging by the front-end damage.

"It's okay, Lindsey. We need to be brave. We're going to have to make a run for it back to the house. Okay?"

"Are you sure, Mommy? It's scary out there. I'm scared."

"We'll be safe there. It's not far," Diana offered, trying to reassure her daughter.

"Okay. Chad will protect us, won't he, Mommy?"

"Yes, honey, he will." Diana knew in her heart it was the truth.

Lindsey climbed into the front seat and Diana took her hand, pulling her out of the car. The rain pummeled them instantly, but without so much as a backward glance, they ran and ran, not stopping until they reached the porch. After saying a silent prayer of thanks, they squeezed the water from their hair and wrung out what water they could from their clothes. Soaked through and through, it was like taking a bath. Only colder.

Knocking on the door, Diana stepped back and pulled Lindsey close as another crack of thunder sounded nearby.

They didn't have long to wait before Chad appeared. "What happened? Get inside quick," he said, pulling Diana forward and making sure they were all inside before he bolted the door shut.

"What on earth are you doing?" he asked.

Diana's emotions had been on a tight lockdown trying to be brave, but now they threatened to escape. She swallowed hard, trying not to break down in front of Lindsey. "You were right. We should have stayed here. A tree came down on the hood of the car. I'm blocking your driveway and I'm not so sure my car is even drivable. It would seem you're stuck with us, I reckon. If the offer is still open, that is," she added, already knowing he would never send her out in the storm.

"Of course it is. Head for the bathroom and I'll look for some of my sister's clothes to see what I can find for you both to wear."

Lindsey wrapped her arms around Chad's leg, soaking him with her wet clothes. Not that he seemed to mind. "I knew you would protect us, Chad," Lindsey said, putting on a brave face.

Chad seemed taken aback by the comment. "For sure."

Once again, Diana was reminded of just how different Silas and Chad were. One lived for himself, the other, well, he was Chad-on-the-spot to help anyone who needed it. It was only natural for Diana to wish for someone more like Chad in her life. Her own personal knight in shining armor.

Chapter Nine

♥

Someone pounding on the door had taken Chad by surprise, knowing Diana had left only ten minutes before. Shock had vibrated through his body as he took in their bedraggled, soaking wet appearance. But her tale of the tree falling...on her car no less, left him reeling. The thought of how close they'd come to a terrible tragedy was not something he could wrap his head around. He wasn't much of a religious man these days, but found himself saying a prayer of thanks to God for keeping them safe and unharmed.

He returned to the living room, a pile of towels in hand. "Here you go," he said, handing them to Diana. "I put several choices of clothing in the bathroom, trying to figure out what could be modified for Lindsey to wear. I'm sure the two of you can figure out what to do, and that anything warm will be welcome."

"You can say that again." Diana let out a deep breath and forced a smile to her face. "Thank you so much." She quickly dried off and then took the towel from Lindsey to begin drying the dripping water from her hair.

"It w...was sc...sc...scary out there," Lindsey said, her teeth chattering. "And that tree...it was a m...monster. It even roared loud as it c...c...crashed to the ground."

"It is a big tree, that's for sure." Diana confirmed her daughter's assessment with a nod.

"I'm so sorry this happened to you both. Thank goodness you're safe. First light, if the rain has stopped, I'll get to work on it by cutting a section of the tree to open up the road. I'll also give Charlie a call and have your car towed to the shop. If there's any hope for it, he'd be the one to fix it. Although Lindsey might be late for school.”

Lindsey brightened, her tiny mouth curving into a smile. “That’s okay, Chad. I’ll have a big story to tell everyone.” Her positive attitude after what she’d just experienced was enlightening.

“While you both get some dry clothes on, I’ll see what I can find for dinner. There might even be some warm cocoa in there, as it was one of Roxanne’s favorite drinks.”

“Sounds good. And th...thanks.” Diana was tense, like a wound-up clock that quit working. Lindsey was moving past the experience far quicker than her mother, it would seem.

Five minutes later, Diana came into the kitchen, surprising Chad with her quick turnaround. “Lindsey’s taking a warm shower. I hope you don’t mind.”

Roxanne’s sweatshirt and sweatpants fit Diana nicely, the two women almost the same size.

From designer jeans to country comfort, and now to baggy lounging clothes, Diana didn't seem the least bit conscious of the change. "Not at all. I should have suggested it myself."

"It's okay. You seem on top of a lot of things." She took the cup of hot chocolate he offered and took a sip. "I should have listened to you when you said not to go. I can't believe how close—" she said, her voice breaking, her eyes welling up with tears.

"What's wrong?" he asked.

Diana brushed at the traces of tears on her cheeks with the sleeve of the sweatshirt. "It's just hard to accept that my foolishness almost got us both killed."

A defeated look crossed her face that broke his heart. Diana was a strong woman, and this had clearly shaken her up. He took the cup from her, set it on the counter and pulled her into his arms, hugging her tight. "Listen to me," he said, tilting her chin up to gaze into her eyes. "You need to stop thinking that way. It wasn't foolishness. You might have made that trip a hundred times in the rain or a storm and nothing would have happened."

"But it did," she whispered, the words ripped from deep within.

Chad wiped a few escaped tears away with the pad of his thumb. "And you're both okay." He had the sudden urge to kiss her, but through sheer will power alone, he resisted.

She closed her eyes and let out a deep breath. "True. Thank you. I need to count my blessings and not fear what might have been. We're safe. And you're here to help us." Her voice was a little stronger, but not quite up to par.

"What else is bothering you?" he asked quietly, digging to the core of truth not yet exposed.

Diana's steadfast gaze pierced him with its intensity. "It's just that I wonder what I would have done if you hadn't been here. I mean, after you head to the city and it's just Lindsey and me. Maybe this is a fool's dream," she said, her voice breaking on the last comment.

"Not so. The Diana I've come to know would call someone to cut the tree and tow the car. I've watched and worked with you for the past week. You're as strong willed and determined as any woman I've ever met. Just trust your instincts."

Diana picked up the mug, clutching it between her hands, almost as if for support. "That's what I did when I left New York. I wanted to find a new home for us. To start over in a place of peace. It's what we needed in our lives, so I let go of my fear of leaving the past and set forth on a new journey."

"Which takes a lot of guts and brings us back to the original point. You can handle anything." Chad shot her a smile, hoping to renew her positive outlook on life.

"Thanks. It's a lot of responsibility knowing I'm solely in charge of Lindsey's life. I just don't want to mess it up."

"You're doing awesome. Lindsey's a great kid. And for the record, I've noticed that since she's been here, she's opening up more, talking more. Seems happier if you ask me." Watching over Roxanne for so many years had taught him how to read the signs, and Diana was more than on the right track with her daughter.

"Mostly because of you. You are so patient with her, especially now with Dawning Light. What's the story with the pony? I mean, is that something people do around here? Lend out their horses?"

Chad shrugged. He didn't want to get into the discussion before, and he preferred not to have it now. Diana could very well get upset about his overture, but he'd done it with the best of intentions. "My friend is selling the pony. I wanted to give Lindsey something special of her own and the pony was perfect. I also remember you telling her when the time was right, she could have one, so you weren't against the idea. I figured the time was right. You get the farm. She gets the pony. I hope you don't mind." He waited, fully expecting her anger at his highhanded generosity.

"No, not at all. It was sweet of you. Although, no more gifts please without talking to me first. The pony is just one more thing to take care of and I'm just trying to figure it all out."

So not upset, which confused him. "I can return Dawning Light if you think it's best. I'm not looking to make things more difficult—just better."

Diana smiled. "And you did, trust me. Your timing was impeccable, as always. Thank you again, and yes, Dawning Light can stay. But you get to tell Lindsey, as you deserve full credit."

Chad shook his head. "Something I don't need or want. I'm not one to be in the limelight." Limelight meant people watching your every move. Something he figured he had enough of in his life without adding more.

"Why is that?" Diana asked.

"Same reason as the milk issue, I reckon. I just want to be left alone and if no one is looking at me, they can't find fault." The conversation had completely sidewinded in a direction Chad didn't want to go.

Diana moved closer and laid a hand on his arm. "But you're a good man. So far, I see no faults, so perhaps the fault is their own."

"Guess it doesn't matter, because talking about it changes nothing. Way past the time for change, which is why I'm headed to the city." Diana had a way of getting him to talk about himself, something no one else could manage to do. He wasn't sure if it was a good thing or a bad thing.

"But won't you miss this place?" she asked, her voice soft and low.

"Yes. I mean, no." He shrugged. "It's confusing. There are parts of this place I love, but more parts I hate." It was like sharing his innermost thoughts with someone. Just who was Diana Gibson Langley?

"Hate is a strong word," she admonished, moving to stand next to the table.

Chad nodded. "It is, but it's a good word when it applies."

"Hate can be poisonous to the soul."

He understood her reasoning, but she didn't understand him. At all. "Unfortunately, there's no antidote for what ails me." Now it really was time for a change in the subject. "How about spaghetti for dinner with a side of garlic bread?"

"Well played diversionary tactic. Spaghetti sounds great, but since you've been so gracious to let us stay, please let me fix dinner. I'll get started right after I check on Lindsey and call over to Serendipity to let them know we're okay and explain why we can't get back there tonight. I wouldn't want Janice to worry."

"Deal." Whether Diana liked it or not, small-town gossips would have a field day with her overnight visit, but her attempt to keep her reputation intact was a good one. Chad turned to leave. "I'll be back in a few. I need to prep the bunk house for me to stay there tonight. Everything you need to for the meal is already on the counter."

"Gotcha. Dinner in thirty minutes, then."

Chad headed for the bunkhouse, grateful for the chance to be alone with his thoughts. Even if it meant braving the pounding rain for a minute or two while he crossed the already soaked yard and jumping around the puddles. He entered, flipped on the lights, and glanced around. Power was good, and no leaks. Another good sign. The hall closet was stuffed with bedding. His phone rang just as he started to pull out the sheets he would need. "Hey, sis. What's up?"

"This storm is what's up. How are you holding up out there? It's miserable here in town, but I've got power," Roxanne said.

She never did like storms. As a child, she used to crawl under the bed and hide until Chad was able to coax her out. "We have power, but a tree came down. Driveway's blocked."

"We?" his sister shot back, zeroing in on his slip.

"Diana and her daughter. The woman I told you who's buying the farm. I've been helping her learn the ropes of dairy farming. They were here when the storm hit. She tried to leave, but the tree came down on the hood of her car. Luckily, they weren't hurt." The image of them standing on the front porch dripping wet, cold, and scared, would haunt him for some time to come.

"Poor dears. There wasn't much warning on this storm, but it's not like you not to know. Never known you to rely on a weather app."

"I was giving Lindsey a pony ride, so I was a little preoccupied."

"Interesting. Perhaps more than a little preoccupied with the girl's mother as well," Roxanne said, connecting her own dots.

Chad shook his head. Not that his sister could see him, but to convince himself. "It's not what you think. I'm only honoring my part of the contract. It was helping her or she walked, and we both know there aren't buyers lined up to buy the property."

"*Hmmm.* If you say so. Sounds like someone I need to meet. Tell me more about her." Roxanne was clearly on one track and wouldn't be derailed.

"There's not much to tell. She's divorced and moving to Crossroads Creek. I'm guessing she likes the fresh country air, since she's moving here from the city."

"Did you show her the fort?" Roxanne asked.

Chad didn't answer. His sister knew the importance of the place, and also that he never took Tonia there. But equally, he wouldn't lie. "Yes. We came across it, that is."

"Wow. I'm impressed. Now I really do want to meet this woman."

"Just stop, Roxanne. It's not what you think. Purely business. I'm city bound and she's a new-country girl. The two can't mix in case you can't work out the logistics on your own," he teased, tossing the bedding on one of the lower bunks.

"Except I'm not convinced you're a city boy. Besides, if you leave, who will make me hot chocolate and fix my booboos?" Roxanne chuckled.

"Time will tell whether you're right or not. And Hank, your husband, has hot chocolate and booboo duty now. This is my life the last time I checked." Chad didn't want his sister coming round the farm and trying her hand at matchmaking.

"Exactly! Which is why you need to stop living in the past. What dad did isn't on us, but you live like it's our sin to bear."

Chad frowned. "Tell that to the folks in town who don't let us forget."

"Not everyone is like that. I have friends here. I've made this my life and I'm happy. You could be too if you let people in. I don't think you'll be happy in the city at all. Not one bit. Six months tops and it will drive you crazy. All the noise and lights. It's not what you're used to on the farm."

They'd had this conversation repeatedly ever since he told her his plans after she announced her engagement to Hank. "Maybe not, but I'll never be happy here either. Maybe I'm cut out to be a drifter."

"Or maybe you're just running from life and need to stop. Accept our past and look for closure. It's what I did, and you can too."

"I've got to run. Diana is fixing supper and I don't want to be late. Stay safe." Chad hung up the phone and shoved it in his back pocket. He lifted his hands to his forehead and began to massage his temples, trying to ease the tension.

Roxanne thought he was running from the past, but he wasn't the only one. Diana was doing the same thing, but in her case, she wasn't an open book and Chad had yet to figure out her story. He valued privacy and didn't pry. Her answer had been to move on, the same thing he was planning to do.

Perhaps they had more in common than either of them knew.

And maybe that's why he felt a connection and the urge to kiss away her tears in the kitchen.

Chapter Ten

♥

THE TEMPERATURE CONTINUED TO rise; the sun beating down on Diana as she pushed the wheelbarrow full of odorific manure and the accompaniment of flies to the side of the barn. After dumping the contents into the compost pile, she used the pitchfork to spread it out the way Chad had shown her. Lindsey was nearby, playing with the chickens, chasing after them. She had a habit of talking to the farm animals like she'd seen in the Dr. Doolittle movie. And her daughter's laughter was a soothing balm to Diana's aching arms and soul, the sound a reminder of why she was doing all this.

Chad had run into town to talk to Charlie about her car. The good news was the damage wasn't as bad as she had expected, and the repairs to get it back on the road would only take a few days. It wouldn't be pretty, but then it was an old car.

As the sun eased downward on the western sky, Diana was more than ready to take a break. "Lindsey, let's head for the house. I picked up some paint the other day and plan to surprise Chad by whitewashing the rockers. The whole place needs a coat of paint, but the front porch is as good a place to start as any."

"Okay," her daughter said, as she came running over. "Did you see me chasing the chickens? I came so close to finally touching one. I must be getting faster." She beamed.

"For sure. You're growing like a weed, Munchkin."

Lindsey scrunched up her face, not liking the comment. "But weeds are bad. I'm not bad, am I, Mommy?"

"No, sweetheart. Like a weed because they grow fast. Not all weeds are bad. Take Dandelions, for instance. They are classified as a weed, but they have many medicinal uses which make them useful. For instance, Dandelions can be used in teas and made into a syrup to help with tummy ache issues."

Her bright smile returned. "Oh, okay then. That sounds way cool."

They stepped onto the porch. The instant relief in the shade brought a welcome change. "Run into the kitchen and grab a snack. I left a banana and an apple on the counter, along with a juicy pouch. You can play inside if you like or stay out here with me and keep me company."

"It's hot out here. I'd rather go inside. Can I watch TV?"

"Sure, but only if Chad has the Discovery Channel, PBS, or Animal Planet. Although he may have none of them," she added.

Lindsey frowned. "But I wanted to watch Nickelodeon."

"That's fine too, if he has it. Otherwise, no TV without supervision. You know the rules." The word cartoon had lost it's meaning over the years, and some kid's shows had far too much adult content or they simply didn't teach good values. It was hard enough raising a child and trying to instill morally sound character traits without having to compete with the media sources using bad behavior as entertainment.

"Fine," Lindsey grumbled, heading inside the house.

One day, her daughter would appreciate the rules, but clearly it wasn't today. Diana picked up the can of paint and the bag with the screwdriver and brushes she'd stashed in the corner earlier. A bit of paint would start the makeover of what was to be her new home, the idea more than appealing as she pictured the entire house with a fresh coat to revitalize it. A light shade of blue with white shutters might be pretty. And with no one else's opinion to consider, it was almost a done deal. That and a few dollars to pay someone to paint the place after the closing on the house. She had no illusions of climbing ladders to do that job by herself.

Picking up the screwdriver, she removed the lid. Using the long stick, she stirred up the contents, blending the separated swirls of black tint. A dab of black tint in white paint went a long way to deepen the color, making it easier to do only two coats. White was always such a finicky color. It was a trick she'd picked up along the way while painting her own bedroom back home. It had been a while since she'd applied her skills, but she looked forward to the end results.

Diana spread out a tarp and moved both rockers onto it. Dipping her brush in the gooey, white paint, she rubbed off the excess from each side of the brush and turned to start on the first rocker. Stroke after stroke, the rocker took on a new life. Almost as though symbolic of her own life. One stroke at a time, she was fixing everything. Painting a new life almost.

She smiled to herself, pleased with her efforts when she stepped back to admire her handiwork. A quick check of her watch revealed it had taken longer than expected to finish both rockers and Chad was due back soon. Diana moved to clean up, closing up the paint cans. Carrying the wrapped brushes inside, she glanced around the room to check on Lindsey, but she wasn't watching TV.

More than likely, she'd grown bored. "Lindsey," Diana called out, not wanting to head down the hall and risk dripping paint.

Her daughter didn't answer.

"Lindsey," she called out a second time, more loudly.

Diana moved to the kitchen and put the brush down in the sink, rinsed off her hands and headed down the hall to check on her daughter.

"Lindsey, I keep calling—" She wasn't in the bathroom, the door hanging open. Diana's heart skipped a beat, momentary concern rushing over her. Moving down the hall, she checked the rest of the house, room by room, calling out her daughter's name. More than a little frantic now, Diana headed outside and searched around the house. *Nothing*.

Chad pulled up to the house and Diana rushed toward him, relieved to have someone who could help her search for Lindsey.

"What's—"

"I can't find Lindsey." They were the words that put terror in every parent's heart. "I mean, I haven't looked everywhere yet, but I have checked the places she should have been, which is in the house. And I've searched around the outside of the house," Diana said, making sure he understood the ground she had already covered.

"The barn?" he asked, his voice tight with tension.

The parent in him resonated with his concern, and it made her feel slightly better. She wasn't overreacting. "I'm headed there now. It's the only place I haven't checked yet. Oh, and I haven't checked the bunkhouse."

"I'm sure she's in one of the two places and fine," he said, taking her by the hand and headed for the barn.

Was he trying to convince her or them both? "I hope you're right. I was painting and got distracted. I should know better, but I thought she was watching TV."

"Relax, Diana, we'll find her. What were you painting?" he asked, as though trying to distract her from going into a frantic worry state.

"The front porch rockers. To make the place look more welcoming and homier."

"Farmer and painter. What other hidden talents do you have?" he asked, pushing open the barn door. "Lindsey," he called out, his voice booming.

Movement by the back door caught Diana's eye. Spotting Lindsey, a rush of relief filled her. "She's over there," Diana said, pointing at her daughter and running over to hug Lindsey.

"What are you doing out here, sweetheart? I told you to stay in the house or come see me on the porch. You didn't have permission to come to the barn alone. I was worried sick when I couldn't find you."

A look of indecision crossed her daughter's face as she looked at Diana and then at the back door of the barn. "I'm sorry, Mommy. I was bored," she said, her big blue eyes brimming with tears.

Diana pulled her daughter into a bear hug. A hug born out of fear and worry, one that only holding Lindsey safely in her arms could cover. She looked up at Chad, noting the relief was echoed in his eyes as well. "It's okay, honey. Just make sure to ask first, so I know what you're doing." She didn't want to cocoon her daughter from life. That is, after all, why she moved faraway from New York in the first place.

"Daddy was here," Lindsey said, dropping a bomb with those three simple words.

Diana sucked in a deep breath, the sickening sensation of nausea threatening to consume her. "What do you mean? He's in New York," she asked, praying Lindsey was speaking of the past. Silas couldn't be here. Not after all they'd done to lose the man from their lives.

"No," she said, shaking her head. "I was playing with the kittens when he came in the barn to talk to me,' she insisted, nervously biting at her lip.

"I see. What did he want?" Diana asked, trying to keep her voice level so as not to scare her daughter. Unlike her own feelings surging through her at the moment. *Silas had found them.* No matter where she went, the feeling he would keep finding her was enough to wipe away any confidence she'd gained. Now was the time to go into protective mode once again. Would the madness ever end? The trust money was to provide for Lindsey, and she'd do whatever it took to keep Silas's grubby hands away from the account.

"He asked who we were visiting here. When I told him it would be our new home, and that you bought the farm, he got really mad. Daddy's scary when he's mad at me."

It broke Diana's heart to hear the words. No child should be afraid of a parent, but unfortunately, the world wasn't always perfect. Not even close. "Maybe you're mistaken, honey. He has no reason to be mad at you," she said, trying to soothe her daughter's hurt.

"His right eye did that weird twitching thing. He was mad all right. I know."

Lindsey had noticed far more about her father than even Diana could have imagined. Thinking she could simply disappear this easily off his radar had been a mistake. One she needed to fix.

"Is he here now? Chad asked, breaking his silence with the question Diana should have asked first.

Her daughter shook her head. "No. Said he had to go and that you wouldn't want to find him here. Told me not to tell you. But I remember, you always said, if someone tells you not to tell, and it's not a happy surprise secret, then it means I should tell you. I don't think daddy being here is a happy surprise. He went out the back door when you came in the front."

"I'm on it," Chad said, gleaming enough information to act, quickly disappearing through the back door.

"Oh, sweetheart," Diana said, lifting her daughter in her arms to cradle her like she did when Lindsey was younger. Lindsey was too smart, something Diana would need to keep in mind. Silas's visit could only mean one thing...the man had tracked her down because he needed more money. Because one thing that was for certain, he'd never wanted his daughter, something he made abundantly clear.

Once again, it was Chad to the rescue. She would be forever grateful to him for handling the situation, as a confrontation with Silas wasn't high on her priority list, especially not with Lindsey right by her side.

"You did the right thing, honey. Telling me. He's your daddy, but things are a bit strained between us and it's my job to keep you happy and safe. I can't do that with him around, not yet anyway. When the time is right for you, I'll make sure you can see him. Deal?" Silas would never hurt Lindsey physically, but emotionally, Diana intended to limit the damage.

"Deal. He's way scary at times, but I still love him. Is that okay?" Lindsey asked.

"Absolutely, honey. Loving someone doesn't have to change, and maybe one day, he won't seem so scary." If Diana had her way, she'd never let Silas see Lindsey again, but it wouldn't be the right thing to do for her daughter. Silas wasn't a good husband, and he was a lousy father, but...he deserved the right to change and be forgiven, for Lindsey's sake. As for Diana, that was a time of her life she couldn't get back, nor did she want to.

The back door opened, sunlight streaming in. Chad crossed to where they waited. "Sorry, but there was no sign of him anywhere."

Diana nodded, unsure whether she was relieved or more worried. They left the barn and headed back to the house. Rounding the front side, all three drew up short when a red convertible mustang skidded to a halt, stirring up dust and gravel. Waving her hand in the air, she tried to clear the dust away, her stomach plummeting as Silas slid out of the driver's side. So much for keeping her problems off the Crossroads Creek radar.

"What do you want?" she ground out, keeping a tight hold on Lindsey's hand, sensing her daughter's tension as she stepped slightly behind Diana. Silas lounged against his vehicle, his cool composure irritating beyond measure. The only satisfaction Diana got was knowing how dusty his designer slacks and shirt were getting.

"Is that anyway to greet your husband?" Silas asked, his snake-like grin chilling.

"Ex-husband," she snapped.

"Close enough. I originally planned to talk to you privately. But now, seeing as it looks like you might be shacking up with a guy and involving my daughter, I didn't think this conversation could wait. Your high and mighty ways aren't looking so high these days if you get my drift."

"Lindsey, run inside. Now." Diana was grateful her daughter did as she was told. This wasn't a conversation for a six-year-old. When the front door closed, Diana turned back to Silas, furious with his disgusting accusations and his sudden appearance. "Nothing could be further from the truth, but your sordid brain would only see what it wants to see. Not that it's any of your business, but this is Chad Thompson, the man who currently owns the dairy farm."

Silas scowled, barely acknowledging Chad. "The dairy farm you're buying from what I hear."

"Using a child to get information is lower than low, but then that explains your own moral compass. And so what? It's none of your business what I do or where I go as of last year. I think it's time you left, as we have nothing to say to one another."

Silas took a step toward Diana. "Aww, but you see, I've reconsidered. I miss my daughter. And us." He scowled in Chad's direction, his easy grin slipping.

Chad took a step closer, the man not one to be intimidated. The move reassured Diana. "Liar. Whatever you want, the answer is no. Now leave," she repeated.

"I think it's time you did what the lady asked, and leave," Chad ground out.

"Stay out of what doesn't concern you," Silas growled, his eye twitching. He turned back to Diana. "I'll go, but you see, there's this little matter of fifty grand that I need, and if you want me to not file for custody of Lindsey...then pay up. Pretty simple deal." He shrugged.

Diana couldn't believe the audacity of the man. Actually, she could. The slime ball was trying to blackmail her for more money. "You don't want custody and you know it. And I'm not paying you another dime." She took a deep breath, trying to control her own anger. Silas had a way of getting to her and making her lose her cool.

"Suit yourself. You always were a spoilsport. But just remember, you've been warned." With his slimy snake grin solidly back in place, Silas pushed the hot button, trying to make her react.

"No judge will give you custody of our daughter now," she snapped, fighting back with the truth.

"Oh, but I think differently. You see, my mother and father are missing Lindsey. One phone call to tell them what you're up to in Crossroads Creek and there'll be plenty of judges ready to side with me. At least back in New York, there are two sets of grandparents as Lindsey's extended family. Here's it just you and new boyfriend."

"You wouldn't dare," she seethed. "There's nothing going on here." The problem was, back in New York, the legal state of their residency still, the courts would likely be swayed by the Gibson family connections. It was like having Mafia connections without the crime ring.

"That's up to the judge, isn't it? Or you and your sizable bank account." He dared to smirk as he delivered the final blow, laying out his blackmail terms clearly.

Chad stepped forward, tension evident in the way he held himself, his jaw tight. Silas, it would seem, had pushed him too far. "We've both told you to leave, and I reckon you ought to be doing just that. This is my property and you're trespassing. If you're not gone in two minutes, I'm calling the sheriff. We'll see how a fancy-pants man like yourself fares in one of our Texan jail cells overnight."

Silas scowled, but kept quiet, the indecision written on his face.

Diana shot Chad a look of gratitude and nodded. It was a case of Chad to the rescue. *Again.*

Silas reached into his pocket and pulled out a set of keys, jangling them as a futile effort to project his indifference. "This isn't over, Diana. Get the money. You know how to reach me."

Silas turned and slid back in his car. The engine roared to life, the man gunning the accelerator to peel out, the tires slipping and shooting dust and gravel in the air, forcing them to jump back.

Royal jerk was the best word she could think of to describe her ex, at least it was if she wanted to honor her faith. Chad remained silent, but his gaze said it all. He wanted answers.

Diana had some explaining to do, but as to how much to reveal, she wasn't sure. Hopefully, Chad would not only understand, but keep the whole affair to himself.

Chapter Eleven

♥

CHAD REACHED DOWN TO grab the gum wrapper that had fallen to the ground when Silas had pulled out his keys. The ex-husband was a litterbug and a fool, but mostly...the word loser came to mind. Following Diana up onto the porch, he shot one last glimpse down the driveway to be sure the man was gone. Only remnants of dust clung to the air, but the whole incident left Chad reeling as they went inside.

Somehow Diana's ex-husband had fully expected her to pony over fifty thousand dollars. Blackmail was an ugly word, but it's exactly what the man was trying to do, using the custody of his daughter as leverage. It turned his stomach to stand by and watch the scene play out, but he'd taken his lead from Diana. However, if the guy had moved any closer to her, it would have been all bets off.

It didn't escape notice that Diana drove a beat-up Buick, and was buying a run-down ranch, not some fancy racehorse farm. Not even close. So why did the man act like she was loaded? The question became...which was the truth and which was a lie? Wealthy and hiding it, or barely getting by and being milked for more money than she had available.

Her manicured nails had long since disappeared as Diana worked the farm, and her fancy haircut had grown out, but nothing could remove the grace in the way she moved and carried herself, or the way she spoke. *Refined.* Which is why he couldn't discount the wealthy and hiding-it option. Which would create a whole other problem for him.

Gossipmongers would have a field day if they realized she was rich, and he was in the picture. He wasn't interested in courting her, or her money, but it wouldn't stop them from speculating. Something to the tune of "the apple didn't fall far from the tree." It wasn't anything different than he'd heard ever since his father was arrested and put in prison for armed robbery. Chad needed to make sure Diana kept the incident to herself and judging by the lack of information she'd volunteered prior to this, he was betting she would agree.

Chad held the door open and allowed Diana to enter first. They needed to talk, not only for the safety of Diana and her daughter, but also to find out what he was up against. He didn't want trouble, but it would seem trouble had landed on his doorstep. "We can talk in the kitchen," he volunteered, not allowing her any room to hold off the inevitable discussion.

"Sure thing. Hey Lindsey, I've got to talk to Chad a minute. Do you mind watching a little more TV before Chad gives us a ride back to the inn?"

"Okay, Mommy. Is he gone? I mean, is daddy gone?" she asked, lines of tension creasing her forehead.

She was just a little girl, and judging by the fierce protective streak in Diana, her ex-husband was a fool to think Diana would ever let him get custody.

"Yes, honey." Lindsey visibly relaxed, making Chad wonder what kind of father could cause that kind of reaction. Clearly not a doting one and someone who couldn't see past his own issues to recognize the effect it was having on his daughter.

They moved off into the kitchen.

Diana turned to him, laying her hand on his arm.

It was a move she did often to get his attention, one that he liked. It was strangely settling.

"Before we have this discussion, I wanted to say thank you. That would not have gone that well without your presence. He's not a nice man when he doesn't get his way," she said.

And just like that, he melted. Whatever bridge they crossed, they'd do it together. He wanted to help her any way he could. "You're welcome. Although, truth be told, I think you would have handled it just fine on your own." The urge to kiss her again hit him out of nowhere, this time requiring more than a little effort not to give in to the pull of attraction. And it was the last thing he should be thinking, especially given the recent turn of events. Not to mention his impending departure. It would be foolish to get mixed up emotionally with anyone—most of all the woman buying the farm.

"Well, I'm glad I don't have to find out. At least he's gone now, even if he is going back to the city to make things difficult for me again." Diana dropped her hand and stepped back, leaving him slightly bereft.

"You've been through this before?" Chad asked.

She nodded. "Unfortunately, yes. When we got divorced. He's not interested in custody of Lindsey," she said in a hushed whisper. "Gambling is his Achille's heel and money is the means to keep him in the running for the next race, waiting for the big win he never seems to get. But it's always the lure of what he might win that keeps him going back for more."

"A true addict who doesn't know when to quit." Her ex reminded him all too well of his own father. A man who wanted money bad enough he'd do anything to get it, including something illegal.

"Exactly. But I refuse to keep paying him. I just want him out of our lives," she said, closing her eyes as though trying to wish the man away.

"Can you afford to pay him?" Chad asked. "Is that why he followed you here?" This was literally the big question...all fifty thousand dollars' worth.

Diana's eyes darkened, the lines across her forehead deepening as she moved toward the door. "That's none of your business."

Chad hadn't expected her to shut down on him. "I disagree. It became my business when the guy trespassed onto my property and threatened you in the process." What was she hiding...and why?

Diana paused, mulling over his words. "True," she said, letting out a deep breath. "Please, promise me this conversation remains between the two of us."

"I'm not a kiss and tell kind of guy." Chad grinned, doing his best to lighten the mood in the kitchen.

Diana shrugged. "We aren't kissing, and I want to make sure there's no telling."

"You have my word," Chad said, knowing there was never any chance he would tell someone.

"The deal is, I do have the money, but it's money for Lindsey's future. And I've already paid him off once, but it was something I had to do, no questions asked. That's how I got full physical and legal custody of Lindsey."

"Sounds like a worthwhile deal to keep it out of court. So why does he think he can show up unexpectedly and demand money?" Chad asked, piecing together the scenario.

"Silas knows there's more money and he won't rest until he gets it all."

"So what's with the subterfuge? The car...the farm."

"We wanted to lay low so Silas wouldn't find us. Wouldn't be able to bother us again. The only way to do that was to reduce the money trail. The problem is, I don't know how he found us, and now, I'm wondering if we need to leave again. I've got to talk to Allison to find out what's going on."

"Running won't solve your problem." The words echoed in his head. Talk about not listening to his own advice. That's exactly what he was doing…running, at least, according to Roxanne.

"Neither will staying. If he follows through on his threat, it could get ugly for Lindsey. I'll do anything to protect her from getting hurt just because her father finds this to be some sort of sick game he can play to extort money."

Their situations were completely different, and yet far too much alike. "If you're right about him, no one would ever award him custody. You said as much already."

"That was for a show of power to Silas, but it's not a chance I'm willing to take." She let out a deep sigh. "There's more to it than I've told you. You see, his parents are more than a little influential in New York City. Along with my parents. Our marriage was arranged as an al-liance between business partners," Diana said, the words filled with bitterness.

"One of those." *Parents with problems*. Chad coined the phrase, wishing there was a group that could help parents find their way back to normalcy, not only for themselves, but mainly for the children. For so many, it was too late.

"Yes, one of those. And the truth is, I was one of them. At least until I finally broke free of the chains." Diana looked away, as though hiding back something from him.

"What happened?" he asked, taking her hand to give Diana the strength to open up to him and share her story.

"My parents gave me an ultimatum. Marry Silas or be cut off. I was fresh out of college with nowhere to go, no job, and no money. Silas and I were sort of friends, though we hadn't spent much time together. We had different friend groups altogether, which should have been a clue what I was getting into. We both knew what was expected of us for the business to be united by family. When the point came, I took the easy way and agreed."

"I see." He didn't, but it sounded good. It's not like this was the dark ages when people arranged marriages.

"Probably not. Most people don't understand the pressure that comes with having to be someone you're not. I hated it, but I was too naïve to fight for what I wanted, or should I say, too afraid to face the challenges of becoming my own person. In hindsight, Allison would have taken me in, I'm sure. But then, she was already working at the company and would have lost her job. I couldn't involve anyone else in my affairs and my grandmother had already passed away years before that."

"So what happened to change everything?" Chad asked, getting a better picture with each passing second.

"Life. Silas wasn't a nice man. I already told you he's a gambler. But add to that drunk, ladies' man, and philandering husband. But those are my words to describe his character. Ask his parents and friends and the term *Golden Boy* comes out every time. So instead of outing him, I left. My parents would have sided with the Gibson's anyway. There's the business, and then of course, wealthy families don't air their dirty laundry."

It broke his heart to see Diana look so defeated. "It sounds like an awful way to live."

She nodded. "It was. I wanted to start over, somewhere fresh and without all the hassles. Silas showing up here has ruined everything."

"Well, he's gone now. Seeing as you called his bluff, I think you stick this out and see what happens. Quit running and establish a life here if that's what you want to do. Don't give him more power to hurt you."

"You may be right." Diana shrugged. "I just don't know. Don't forget, you promised not to breathe a word of this to anyone."

Time to be a little more truthful considering all that Diana had shared. "Trust me, I don't want this to get out either. I've told you before

I don't like to be the object of idle conversation and gossiping tongues."

"Why is that? You're a tough guy and I can't believe you'd let them say anything that would bother you. Unless...this is about why you sell your milk a couple of towns away, isn't it?" Diana asked, zeroing in on the issue.

"Smart and beautiful. Potent combination," he added, flashing her a smile. "Yes. And though I'm leaving, I don't want anything to upset my sister and her new marriage. She's happy here and I hope for her sake, it stays that way. The sooner I'm gone, the better it will be for her in the long run."

"Do you want to talk about it?" she asked.

Chad shook his head. "Not really."

"I told you about my ugly past. How much worse can it be?" she quipped, turning the entire conversation to focus on him.

"I don't think comparing notes will do us any good. But I am more than a little curious why *you* don't want people in town to find out?"

"The last thing I want is for people in town to start treating me differently because I have a little money. For the first time in my life I want to be liked for me," Diana said, the confidence returning to her voice.

"I liked you before I found out," he teased, shooting her a wink.

"That's news to me, cowboy."

"My secret is out." Chad moved closer, unable to resist the draw between them. Both had their private life issues, but both were trying to take control and move forward.

Diana's eyes grew wide in surprise at his near-ness. "Can you give us a ride back to the inn? I've got to call my friend back home and see what she knows. It's always best if I can stay a step ahead of Silas, and I definitely didn't manage to do that this time."

"Not a problem." He reached out to brush a lock of hair back from her face. "It'll be okay, you'll see," he added. He liked Diana and truly wanted her to succeed with the farm. He also didn't want to risk her walking away from the contract, as it was his ticket out of Crossroads Creek.

But mostly, in that moment, he still wanted to kiss her. Chad leaned forward intent on capturing just a taste, lost in the moment.

"Mommy," Lindsey called out loudly from down the hall. "The remote stopped working and I can't find the PBS channel."

"Coming, sweetheart." Diana stepped back, a look of indecision on her face. She'd clearly felt the same way he did, including the ambiguity of what to do about the feelings growing between them.

After getting Lindsey squared away with the remote, Diana called Allison, surprised when she answered on the first ring.

"Hey, bestie. You are just the person I need to talk to. Must have read my mind all the way from Texas," Allison teased.

"Actually, I wanted to ask you about Silas. Nothing less glamorous than that."

"Tell me about it. I just left the phone shop because I was having issues with my cell phone, and you'll never guess what he found. An incoming ping tracker malware app. Any clue who might have put it there?" she asked, the tone of her voice all too clear on who she suspected would do something so devious.

"Silas." Diana let out a deep breath. At least that explained how he found them at the Thompson farm.

"Right in one guess. Dirty rat."

Diana rubbed at her temples trying to massage away some of the tension. "That's what I was calling to tell you. Silas was here. He talked to Lindsey secretly and then tried to blackmail me for more money.”

“This guy needs to be in jail.” Allison never liked Silas, her friend an excellent judge in character.

Diana nodded. “I totally agree.”

“So how were things left?” Allison asked.

“Chad sent him packing or threatened to have him arrested for trespassing.” Diana still remembered Silas’s outraged expression with a sense of satisfaction.

“Too bad your cowboy friend didn’t do it anyway. The idea of Silas rotting in a jail cell overnight gives me great pleasure.”

Diana chuckled. “You and me both. But I haven’t seen or heard anything from him since he left. You?”

"Silas hasn't been back in the office either. I'll keep poking around and see what I can find out."

"Just be careful," Diana warned, worried about her friend.

"Will do. You, too. Oh, and say hi to your hunky hero cowboy for me," Allison teased.

"He's not my cowboy."

"But he could be."

"Later." It was better not to go down this road with Allison because she wasn't convinced Diana's swearing off men was the right thing to do. She wanted happily-ever-after for all of her friends.

Chapter Twelve

♥

It had been a long but successful week, and Diana felt some of the tension slipping from her body. Hard work had a way of doing that for a person. The days of aching muscles were smoothing out as she grew more accustomed to the demands of dairy farming.

So far, there still hadn't been a peep from the Silas family camp, nor from her parents. Diana wasn't sure if that was a good or bad sign.

Lindsey was flourishing at school, and they were only two weeks away until the closing on the farm. Diana's new life and future were just around the corner. As she and Chad worked together, an easy camaraderie had surfaced, and it was rather nice having him around all the time. More than nice, not that she'd tell anyone. It was her little secret.

The idea of leaving had been a knee-jerk reaction to want to flee the area and go somewhere Silas wouldn't find them. But she also knew, more than anything, she wanted to stay in Crossroads Creek and make this her new home. The people in town were welcoming and friendly to her and Lindsey, something they needed. *A place to belong.*

Diana looked up as Chad entered the barn. "Hey, I'm going to run into town and over to the vet's place to pick up the medicine we need for the sick heifer. I'll need to take your truck, of course," she said. Chad hadn't complained about the extra work of playing chauffeur to her and Lindsey, but then he clearly felt guilty her car was put out of commission by the falling tree on his property.

Chad nodded and tossed her the keys. "That sounds good. While you're at it, see about getting your own truck," he offered, shooting her a grin.

"Oh, but yours is such a work of art with its rusted fenders," she teased. "*Not*. I'll look into it, but Charlie said my car would be ready in a few days." She had already dropped by the car lot in town and found the truck she wanted, but for the time being had kept the information to herself. Diana would prefer not to finance it, not liking the idea of interest and payments. But the truck was new enough that it came with a hefty price tag. People didn't tend to have that kind of cash lying around and it would draw attention she didn't want.

"Two weeks will be over in no time at all, Diana. Don't put everything off until it's too late," he warned.

"Yes, boss." She grinned. What she needed was a story to cover her tracks. Perhaps a gift from her parents. Good story, but a lie nonetheless, and something she wouldn't do. Or simply take her chances and pray no one cared to talk about it. Diana laid the rake against the wall. "Later," she said with a wave. Spinning back toward the door, she suddenly found herself sailing through the air as she tripped over a bale of hay. Putting out her hands, she cushioned the fall.

Chad rushed to her side. "Are you okay?" he asked, offering his hand for assistance.

She frowned, color burning her cheeks. "Do I look okay? Why on earth was the hay there?" she snapped, not because she was angry...more so, embarrassed.

"I just carried it in. That is the usual way hay ends up in the barn. It's sitting here because you waylaid me for the keys."

Diana grasped his hand, all too ready to get back on her feet and end the humiliation of falling in the first place. "Very funny, wise guy. You could have warned me." As she stood, Diana came toe to toe with Chad, his cologne pleasantly enveloping her. Her awareness of him was on heightened alert and she made a move to step away, except Chad hadn't let go of her hand.

"I was about to, if that count's for anything," he murmured, picking a few pieces of straw from her hair.

Diana stilled. This was Chad. The man selling her the farm and leaving in two weeks, but she couldn't help the feelings surging through her. The two of them were connected in an odd sort of way, the bond stronger after the run in with Silas. It was obvious Chad was sensing the same thing as he stood there, gazing down at her, an odd expression on his face.

"Thank you," she murmured, brushing off her jeans of some imaginary dust to avoid his inquisitive eyes.

"You're welcome. Tell you what. Why don't we go into town together and pick up the meds? Then we can head over to the dealership and find something suitable. I'll make sure you get a good deal."

"*Ummm*, I need to confess something. I've already found a vehicle. But it would be great if you could look it over. I'm not exactly knowledgeable about the pros and cons of picking out a truck."

"Interesting, and you didn't want to tell me. Let me guess, something small, short bed, and purple," he teased.

Diana grinned. "Not quite." Diana stepped back and the two of them headed for the truck.

Chad drove into town and parked in front of the vet's office. "Sit tight, I'll be right back." "I was going to pay for meds since they are to keep my cows healthy," Diana said, knowing Chad was on a tight budget but not wanting to step on his dusty boots.

Deep lines formed across Chad's forehead, his frown an echo of displeasure. "We've talked about this before. Until the place is yours, it's still my responsibility. A man has his pride, you know."

It was no more than she figured and not worth arguing about. "Fine. I'm just trying to be neighborly," she offered to smooth things over.

"We aren't neighbors. Business associates is more like it." Chad shut the door and headed inside.

Business associates was not the term she would have used. Friends. *Good friends*. It was true. Over the past weeks, they had become close, each giving support when and where needed. Lindsey had also formed a bond with Chad. On more than one occasion she had asked why Chad had to move away. But it was the second half of her daughter's question that was way more difficult to answer. The part where she asked why they couldn't all live at the farm. *Together*.

Something that would never happen. Once or twice the thought had crossed Diana's mind, but the reality always shut down those wayward thoughts. She wasn't looking for love, and neither was Chad.

Love complicated life in a way she didn't need.

Five minutes later, Chad returned, tossing a small white bag on the front seat. "We can walk over to the car lot from here if you want."

"Works for me," she said, sliding out of the truck. They crossed the street and walked to the end of the block, cutting the corner of the lot to make their way to the area where the trucks were parked.

"This one," Diana said, stopping behind the truck she'd picked out.

Chad let out a low whistle. "Wow. You don't mess around, do you? And a Chevy at that. I'm kind of partial to that make. A 3500 is a lot of truck, but it looks like a sweet ride. You've got good taste."

"I realize it's a lot of truck, which is why I want to take a test drive. See how it feels and make sure it's a good fit for me. Interested?"

"Wouldn't miss it." Chad grinned. "You are full of surprises Diana Langley."

"Thank you. What a lovely compliment."

Chad walked around the truck, checking it over. "So why didn't you buy it the other day when you were here?"

"I didn't have time to do the paperwork for a loan."

"Why would you...never mind. You might be taking things a bit far, but I reckon it's your life and your decision. You've got time now. Let's take it for a test drive, and then if you still want to buy it, you can do the paperwork. I've been meaning to visit Roxanne, but the past couple of weeks have been super busy."

Busy because of her. "Sounds like a good plan. I wonder if the owner of the lot will do anything with my car when it's fixed."

"Doubtful. That thing is more than likely junk-yard material at this point."

"It's not that bad," Diana insisted. Secretly, she hated it, but it was the car she'd chosen for a specific purpose. One that had served her well until now. Which wasn't the car's fault at all.

"Yes, it is." Chad grinned, his easy smile curling her toes with the warmth. Someone to laugh with had always been a character trait she wanted in a husband. A trait Silas was seriously lacking. "When you finish up here, we could meet back up for lunch before you need to pick up Lindsey."

"Sounds like a good plan." Time off from the farm. Diana remembered Chad saying there was never any, but so far, it seemed like there were more than ample opportunities to have down time. Team work it would seem got the job done. "We don't get to eat in town much, so it will be a nice change."

"Agreed. And the company is good." He shot her a wink. "Hey, Victor," Chad said, greeting the man who owned the lot.

The two men shook hands. "I'm surprised to see you here. You always said you would never part with your truck. Finally making sense and decide to get a new one?" the man asked eagerly, sensing a sale on the horizon.

Middle-aged, balding, and rather thick around the middle, he seemed pleasant enough.

"No, but Diana is in the market," Chad said, nodding in her direction.

Victor turned to her, his reaction one of surprise. "That's a mighty big truck. Maybe something smaller would suit you better."

Her opinion of Victor dropped considerably. "And maybe you should let me be the judge of that." She hadn't meant to sound off so sharply, but after the way Silas and all the parentals treated her as if she were a commodity, she was through with people telling her what she could and couldn't do, and more so, what she could or couldn't buy. Chad might have originally teased her about wanting something small and easy to handle, but he hadn't made the mistake of trying to talk her out of something she wanted.

"Sorry, ma'am, I wasn't trying to offend you," he offered, a guilty expression on his face.

It was old school to think men were more suited to big trucks than women. Hopefully, as a car dealership owner, he wouldn't make the mistake again. "None taken." She shot him a smile to back her words. It wasn't his fault she'd learned to stand up for herself the hard way and was a bit defensive.

"Diana wants to take it for a test drive," Chad interceded.

"Great. I'll get the keys." Victor moved off, leaving them alone.

"Seems you aren't the only one who has preconceived notions about me," she teased. "First about the farm, and then let's face it, it's not the truck you painted a picture of for me."

"But I quickly changed my mind about you. So did he." Chad grinned, shooting her a conspiratorial wink.

Another warm and fuzzy rush shot through her. She loved his sense of humor...and then those winks of his...they could melt a woman's heart. "I didn't realize you were in my fan club now?"

"Absolutely. You've proven you're more than capable of handling the farm. You're hardworking and dedicated, a great combination for the new venture of yours."

"Spoken by the guy trying to unload the place," she teased.

A thoughtful expression crossed his face. "It wasn't always that way. When I was younger, I loved the farm. Life has simply shown me over the years that it's not for me. Just like life is showing you the opposite. We all have our strengths and weaknesses, and my weakness is the farm."

Chad opening up to her and revealing some of his innermost thoughts was a new experience, and it made her want to do the same. "And my weakness is being controlled…by anyone. So there you have it. Now, how about this truck?"

"Let's find out." Chad spent the next few minutes under the hood, checking out the engine. "Looks good, but I'll know more on the test ride." He crawled under the truck. Not anything she would have thought to do.

"What are you checking for?"

"Rust. Making sure the truck isn't from a place that uses heavy salt on the roads. Tends to rust out the undercarriage quicker than it should," he explained.

"Good thought, and not one I would have considered. Thanks for doing this."

Scooting back out from under the truck, he sat up. "It's my pleasure. And no issues on that front either. Chassis looks good."

Whatever that meant. Diana was sure it had something to do with the undercarriage considering that's what Chad had inspected. And good was golden in her books. They both turned as Victor approached.

Diana took the keys from Victor as he held them out to her. "Thank you. We won't be gone long."

"Take whatever time you need. I'm not going anywhere," Victor said.

"Can you run her a VIN check while we go on the test ride?" Chad asked.

"I actually already have one on file. I'll pull it for you."

Diana moved to the driver's side and pulled open the door. It was quite a bit heavier than her car door, but to be expected. She hoisted one foot up and, using the frame of the truck, tried to pull herself up using the door. And failed. She tried again and failed. A heated warmth flushed her cheeks as Chad came around, sensing the issue she was having. "*Ummm*, maybe the truck is too big, if I can't even get in it."

"You'll be fine. That's what the handle is for when you're a bit...shorter than some folks." He grinned. "Put your right foot on this molding." He pointed to the wide plastic strip that lined the driver side floor board. "Grab the steering wheel with your right hand, this handle with your left. Then shove off the other foot and pull yourself in."

She followed his instructions, terrified of falling flat on her keister in front of him. She'd already done that once today.

Except it didn't happen. He was right, and it worked. "Thank you," she said, suddenly feeling on top of the world. *Literally*. Sitting this high up in a vehicle was nothing she'd ever experienced.

"You're welcome." He closed the door and went around to the other side.

Diana started the engine. "Sounds good, right?" The motor hummed with a raw sense of power. One she really liked.

Chad chuckled. "It does at that. Diesel engines are loud, but combined with the size of this truck, and this comes a lot closer to a monster truck.

The test ride lasted all of ten minutes, and Diana was sold. "I love it," she exclaimed.

"Good news. I don't see any reason the VIN report will have any issues considering this is a newer vehicle, so I reckon you've got yourself a truck," Chad said.

"Yay." He seemed genuinely happy for her...but then he wouldn't have to cart her around town anymore.

They headed back to the car lot and finalized the negotiations with Victor, the man over-the-top pleased to have made a sale.

"The paperwork will take about forty-five minutes or so. There's one other sale ahead of yours, but I can get you started filling out forms," Victor offered.

"That works." Diana couldn't believe it. She was really buying a truck. The financing option wasn't her personal preference, but it was all part of what she needed to do to fit into the community. Flashing money around wouldn't buy her friends around Crossroads Creek. Or it might, which is something she was determined to avoid.

"I'll head to my sister's as planned. Just give me a call when you're done and we can stop at Courtney's Deli for lunch. Lindsey will be thrilled with the new ride home. I mean to the farm," Chad corrected.

Home sounded much better. To her anyway. "Works for me. And yes, she will. Especially being so high up in the quad cab, she'll be able to see everything."

"Later," Chad said, waving a hand in farewell as he headed down the sidewalk.

More than an hour and a half later, the paper-work was finally finished. Diana was going to cut it close for her to pick up Lindsey. After the first hour had passed, she'd given up all hope of meeting up with Chad for a late lunch. Diana had called to cancel, and since she had a ride home, he didn't need to wait anymore. When he didn't answer, she left him a message, hoping he would get it before too long.

As she pulled out of the dealership and turned left to head for Lindsey's school. Diana was surprised to see a lot of folks in town gathered out on the street, the crowd growing quickly as others came rushing to join. Curious, she edged closer and noticed the flashing blue lights of two police cars that blocked Main Street from either direction.

She came to a stop and rolled down the window. "What's going on?" she asked one of the people heading toward the group.

"The bank was robbed about a half hour ago. Folks are in a tizzy," the old man said, pushing his spectacles back to look closer at Diana.

"Oh no." Diana had hoped to leave the crime behind when she left the city, but it would seem that hadn't happened. "Was anyone hurt?"

"Nope. Man said he had a gun, but no one saw it. They're talking to witnesses now. People in town are pretty shaken up. Hasn't happened since..." His eyes grew wide and stopped talking. "I've got to go."

Diana would have liked the man to finish his sentence. Whatever it was, must have been pretty important for him to rush off.

She turned around and headed for the school, where Lindsey waited outside at the pickup lane. One of the last to get picked up, Diana could tell her daughter was in a sour mood. At least she was until she saw the truck, her face brightening when she recognized the driver.

"Is this ours?" Lindsey asked, a hopeful look on her face.

"It is. Do you like it? It took longer than expected getting the paperwork done, so I'm sorry if I'm a little late," Diana offered by way of explanation.

"I love the truck. And it's okay being late for this." Lindsey grinned.

"Here, let me help you get up inside," Diana said. "I'll have to see about adding some steps. I've seen them on trucks before. Might make it easier for both of us." She laughed.

It was a short drive back to the farm, and as she pulled in, she noted Chad was already back. He must have gone straight to work because his Chevy was parked beside the barn. Diana slid out of the truck, helping her daughter down. Lindsey started to run ahead but stopped, turning back to her. "I'm going to go see Chad and the animals. Okay?" her daughter asked.

"Sure thing. I'll just run into the—" Sirens filled the air. Diana spun around. Heading down the driveway, dust flying, were two police cars, blue lights flashing as they skidded to a halt.

The sheriff got out of the car, followed by the other two policemen. Weapons drawn, but luckily not pointed. They were headed in Diana's direction, scaring the daylights out of her. She grabbed Lindsey's hand and held tight as the men approached.

"Chad here?" the sheriff asked, his gaze scanning the area.

What could they possibly want with Chad? "He's in the barn, I think. We just got back. Is everything okay?"

"No, ma'am, it's not. The bank in town was just robbed and Chad's our lead suspect. We're here to arrest him. You best go on inside and wait."

No way. They had it all wrong. Not her Chad. Except he wasn't her Chad. "There must be some mistake," she said as two of the officers headed for the barn.

"No mistake. You're new around here, but we know what we're doing. There is more than enough coincidence in an old case for us to bring Chad in for questioning. Looks like a copycat robbery. For your sake, you should stay out of this."

Lindsey tugged at her arm. "Mommy, why do they want to arrest Chad? He's not a bad man."

"I'm sure it's just a mistake, honey. Let's do as the sheriff asks and head inside." She led Lindsey toward the house, more than a little concerned, but wanting to shield her daughter from what was happening.

They'd gone to town together, but he hadn't been with her the whole time. In fact, he had gone to visit his sister while the bank was being robbed. The question was...did he really go to his sisters? *Copycat robbery*. She didn't have a clue what the sheriff was talking about, but doubt assailed her. Glancing over toward the barn, she was shocked to see the two uniformed men leading Chad out of the barn.

In handcuffs.

Chapter Thirteen

♥

"YOU'RE MAKING A HUGE mistake," Chad snapped, glaring at the officer who felt duty bound to keep one hand glued to Chad's arm. As if their "prime suspect" would get far with handcuffs and two lawmen to stop him. Their words...not his. Words that rubbed him the wrong way, considering he was innocent.

Make that three lawmen. Sheriff Jones was talking to Diana.

Chad's blood boiled at the sight, more so when she looked his way, turned, and led Lindsey into the house, without so much as a backward glance. And it was still his house...at least it was for two more weeks.

The fact she didn't say anything to him more than signaled the truth as to her feelings. She believed the sheriff and his cronies, her rejection proof she figured he was guilty.

"What were you doing in town this afternoon, Chad?" Sheriff Jones asked when they reached the patrol cars.

"I was helping Diana buy a truck. And I stopped at the vet's office to pick up medication for one of the cows. You all are making a mistake. Same old story. Something happens in town and blame it on the thief's son." Chad was sick and tired of the story and paying for his father's sins. The sooner he left Crossroads Creek and never looked back, the better. But first, he had to clear his name, or they'd throw him in jail and toss away the keys.

"So you say. But we got folks seeing your truck parked for quite a while near the bank. But from what I hear, you didn't visit the bank, least not for regular banking. And you weren't with Diana the whole time. Victor said you left the dealership around one. No one seems to be able to account for your presence until almost two. The bank was robbed at two-twenty."

The man was roughly five foot five, and what he lacked in height he tried to compensate for with meanness. His wide stance wasn't the least bit intimidating, but the power he held...well that counted for a lot.

"I was at my sister's house."

"And she can verify that?" Sheriff Jones asked.

"Well, no." Chad frowned, not liking the direction this was headed. "She wasn't home, so I was waiting to see if she would show up while I waited for Diana to finish filling out her loan paperwork at the dealership."

The sheriff's gaze hardened. "*Hmmpphh.* In other words, no alibi."

What ever happened to innocent until proven guilty? "You can check my phone records. I sent a text to Roxanne that I was there, asking where she was at."

"That don't make a clean alibi. You have the right to remain..."

Chad felt as though he were suffocating. His head was spinning and everything was a blur, including the words as the sheriff read him his rights."

"You're being charged with armed bank robbery and it's time to head to the station. Get in the car," the sheriff said, taking control of directing Chad into the back seat with a more than necessary firm pressure.

It was enough to snap Chad out of the fog. "Just because my old man robbed a bank doesn't automatically mean I would do the same thing," he seethed.

The sheriff shrugged. "No, but the fact it was a copycat robbery sure points all directions at you. Meet you two back at the station," he told the others.

"Copycat?" Chad asked, not liking the sound of what he was hearing. Surely someone could verify his whereabouts.

The sheriff headed down the driveway, glancing up briefly in the rearview mirror. "Yup. Barged in through the front door with a blue ski mask. Waved a gun in his pocket and shouted for everyone to get down on the floor. Passed a note that said, *'give me all the cash in your drawer or you ain't going home breathing tonight.'* Then the man left out the employee door and fled on foot. Sound familiar?" Sheriff Jones ground out, his eyes tight with hate.

Familiar was an understatement. Chad knew the story well, as it was his father's story.

The sheriff shook his head. "Would have thought you'd be smarter than that, but then robbing a bank ain't all that smart to begin with."

"Except I didn't rob a bank. What if someone is trying to frame me?" he asked, grasping at straws.

The sheriff looked back at him again, a thoughtful expression on his face. "Any enemies here in town?"

Chad thought about it long and hard. "No. I keep to myself. For a reason. Unless you count the people who hate my old man, which is just about everyone."

"Well then, no specific enemies. Can't go accusing the whole town. So, no motive for me to look elsewhere. We never did find that hat, but I reckon we might now," the sheriff said, a little too eagerly for Chad's liking.

At the jailhouse, the walk of shame into the station felt as though he were being led to a guillotine. One thing he learned over the years was that in life, there were no guarantees. And right now, that meant there was always a chance he wouldn't be cleared of a crime he didn't commit. Not when the arresting officers had a grudge.

Officer Larry Balding did the headshot honors as Officer Lawson started the paperwork.

"Don't I get a phone call?" Chad asked. He had to let Roxanne know what was going on and see if her husband could talk some sense into someone. Anyone. The man did have connections in town and as much as Chad didn't like owing people anything, this was the time to break his own rule and ask for help.

"Sure thing." Officer Lawson nodded, pushing a desktop phone in his direction.

So much for privacy. Chad called his sister, relieved when she answered.

"Hey, there. Sorry I missed you at the house," Roxanne said.

Chad let out a deep breath. "Me too, for more reasons than you know."

"Why? What's up? Did you hear the bank was robbed this afternoon?" she asked.

"Oh, I heard all right, right before they read me my rights. They've arrested me and I'm being charged with armed bank robbery." It was like some kind of nightmare, but he couldn't wake up.

"Arresting you?" she snapped. "How can that be? Did you tell them they've got the wrong man?"

"I tried, but they are biased and don't want to listen." He glared at Officer Lawson, not caring that he was maligning the very people processing him into the system.

"That's ridiculous. You were at my place, weren't you?"

"Of course. They say I have no alibi for two-twenty, and since the job was pulled off in copycat fashion to dad's robbery, it makes me their number one suspect."

"I'll talk to Hank. This is all wrong and you're not dad." The anguish in her voice was unsettling, as he'd always tried to protect his little sister...from everyone.

And now, in a role reversal, he needed her help. "Tell that to the sheriff."

"What about your cell phone location? Surely it pinged a tower when you texted me."

"Sheriff said it wouldn't prove anything, as I can leave a phone wherever I want and the timing only requires a short window of opportunity." Secret code for...you did it and I'm taking you down. Revenge well played but oh, so wrong.

"Maybe not, but it's a shadow of a doubt, and he needs to make sure they get the right guy. Not just the easiest guy to make them look good," she huffed.

"Times up," Officer Lawson said, pressing the disconnect button on the phone.

Roxanne had a point. Hopefully, his sister would visit him in jail because there was a lot more that needed to be said. And he needed to give her power of attorney to sign the real estate documents just in case he wasn't available for the meeting. He didn't want anything to stop the sale.

Thinking of Diana and her forlorn expression was more than enough to sober his anger at the situation. In fact, it drained him of all feeling. Diana's opinion meant much to him, probably more than anyone else he knew. They'd grown close, and the thought of kissing her stronger, but he'd held back. Now he was glad he'd done so. Getting involved with Diana would have complicated things beyond measure, and something like this would have ended it anyway.

She'd turned her back on him just like everyone else he knew. Roxanne was all he had for family and unfortunately, he was having to drag her through the mud with him on this one. Never again.

Officer Lawson led him down the hall, the cell keys dangling on a ring he twirled, the jingling sound more than a little daunting. It was just like in the movies, only this was a channel he couldn't turn off.

"Make yourself comfortable. It's going to be a long night. And once the judge signs off on the arrest warrant, well then you'll be here until your court date. I'm sure the judge will agree you're a flight risk."

"Check the phone records and get the ping location. It will put me at my sister's place."

"The sheriff already said he'd look into it. Takes time to do things, so you'll just have to wait this one out."

The man didn't have to be so happy about locking him in the cell. But then Lawson's daddy was another one of the men in the bank the day his father robbed it.

·❤·❤·❤·❤·❤·

Chad's head throbbed from a horrible night spent tossing and turning. It was worse than he could have imagined. Small town, small jailhouse. A cell that made him feel as though he were trapped in nothing more than an oversized dog house. The bed was nothing more than a cot with a blanket. He longed for the wide-open spaces of the farm. Which came as quite a surprise, considering he was bent on selling and heading for the city.

Voices travel down the hallway, alerting him someone other than the jailor was in the building. It wasn't long after that, Sheriff Jones appeared, his expression tight. Someone put the man in a bad mood this morning.

Chad moved to stand at the cell door, gripping the iron rods until his fingers were a bloodless white. Better to transfer his negative energy to something that wouldn't break. "Any news on getting me out of here for something I didn't do?" he asked, taking advantage of the opportunity to push his innocence.

Sheriff Jones shook his head, looking none too pleased. "Unfortunately, you were right. Your cell phone pinged at your sister's place and the judge says I can't hold you without more evidence."

Thank you, Lord. "Sorry to disappoint you. Figured you would be more interested in justice than personal persecution. My father and I are not the same person. It's a shame you can't see that, to the point you would prosecute an innocent man."

The sheriff scowled as he unlocked the cell. "I didn't say you were innocent. I said I couldn't hold you any longer. You may be free to go, but it's only temporary. Stick around town, son. I plan to keep an eye on you and get the evidence I need to pick you up again. It's not like you couldn't have gone to your sister's, walked to the bank, pulled off the job, and then walked back to her house. Probably hid the money somewhere nearby. That's my theory. And if I find out your sister's involved, you're both going to jail. Mark my words." His steely-eyed gaze bore into Chad like a jackhammer.

"There won't be evidence because I didn't commit the crime. And you're wasting time that could be better spent tracking down the real bank robber. That's something that won't look good when it comes time for reelection." Chad had voted for the man...perhaps out of guilt. But it wouldn't happen again.

"It's all good. The people in town know the truth. They haven't forgotten your daddy. Eventually, someone will get me the information I need to haul you back in."

The truth was, the people in town *hadn't* forgotten. And this latest development would have set tongues to wagging in a fresh wave. And there was no way to protect his sister from the backlash. Chad couldn't get out of there fast enough, and he turned to leave.

"Don't forget...stick around town," the sheriff warned.

"You know where to find me." *At least for the next two weeks. After that, he wasn't making any promises.*

Chapter Fourteen

♥

DIANA STILL COULDN'T BELIEVE Chad had been arrested for the armed robbery yesterday. All night long, images of him being led off in hand-cuffs plagued her. In the time she had spent getting to know him the past couple of weeks, she never would have expected him capable of anything like this. But if the locals were to be believed, Chad's past was certainly playing a role in his future. *A future in prison.*

Even with Lindsey by her side, townsfolk spoke freely about Chad's father and that long ago fateful day when he had chosen to rob the bank at gunpoint. But then killing the sheriff, acci-dentally or otherwise, and terrorizing people who had the misfortune of being in the lobby that morning would be something hard to forget.

All information Chad had refused to discuss with her.

Throw in the knowledge Chad sold his milk two towns over because of the ill will towards him in Crossroads Creek, and it all made sense. Over the years, it would seem Chad was being blamed for his father's sin. Except now, it would seem with good cause. The words copycat robbery would forever ring in her head. Between that and his unknown whereabouts at the time of the robbery, Chad was their prime suspect, not to mention their only suspect, if the sheriff was to be believed.

But how much of the ill will was because Chad's father died in prison of a heart attack, Diana didn't know. It was clear some people felt the sentence was never carried out, and that they were cheated of justice. Death in itself, should have been the end. One thing was for certain, anyone who still believed the sins of the father had to be borne by the son, needed to look into their own hearts and have a talk with God. The Lord loves righteous men and women who believe in Him and follow His ways...forgiving all the trespasses of one's parents.

The other, she discovered, was that not the whole town felt the same way. Some people cared about Chad and Roxanne and the injustices done to them. They were the ones calling for a better investigation. It definitely made for a tense room at breakfast this morning in the diner.

But as to her, Diana wasn't positive where she landed on the subject. She wanted Chad to be innocent, believed in her heart he had to be, but...could she trust him?

What if his sudden interest and kindness to her was because he had found out about her money and saw her as a ticket to a better life? It wouldn't be the first time she'd encountered people who would stoop that low. And falling short of that, would he rob a bank? The man did need money. Lots of it.

Something wasn't adding up and her own personal jury was still out, but either way, life in Crossroads Creek had become more than she bargained for. She couldn't risk getting hurt or involved, even more so because she needed to protect Lindsey at all cost.

Her daughter wouldn't like what she was about to do, but Diana felt like there was no other choice but to leave Crossroads Creek. *Contract or no contract*. The dairy farm was not the home for them. Between Silas's appearance and Chad's troubles, leaving town seemed like the most sensible thing to do. Only Lindsey would have a problem with being uprooted again.

Not an entirely true statement she realized. Diana would truly miss this place. Specifically, the farm. In a few short weeks, she'd learned so much and felt a connection with the place, knowing it would be hers. More specifically, although why with what she knew, she couldn't begin to fathom, she would miss Chad. His handsome grin and winning ways had grown on her. Her heart said Chad was innocent, but since when could she trust her heart?

"Eat up, Lindsey. We've got lots to do this morning. I've come to a decision and I hope you'll trust me." After dealing with Silas, the last thing she wanted for her and Lindsey was another man in their life they couldn't trust. One who would land trouble at their doorstep.

"What is it, Mommy?" Lindsey asked, her fork stopping half way to listen.

"As you know, Chad got arrested yesterday."

"For that bank robbery, right? There's no way it was him," she said, folding her arms across her chest in defiance.

"Probably not. But we aren't the police and it's their job to find out. Meanwhile, I think it's best we look for a new home," Diana said, steeling herself for the outcry.

Lindsey's eyes welled up with tears. "Nooo," she whined. "I like it here. Please, Mommy. I don't want to move again." Her lower lip trembled.

Diana reached out to take her hand. "Honey, I'm sorry. But with all of Chad's legal trouble, I think it's for the best. There's just so much that's happened that leads me to believe this isn't where we belong." She was trying to convince her daughter as much as she was trying to convince herself.

"And because daddy found us?" Lindsey asked, her forehead scrunched tight in a thoughtful frown.

Her daughter was too smart for her own good. The truth was better than fiction, but how did one malign their father? *You didn't.* "Your dad went back to New York. Everything will be fine on that accord." That is, if he didn't follow through with his blackmail attempt, but that wasn't something she'd ever let Lindsey find out about.

Lindsey's shoulders slouched as she let out a deep breath. "Okay, Mommy. Johnny stuck his tongue out at me in school yesterday, so maybe we should go."

Poor Lindsey. Her comment proved all the more reason why they should stick around. How else would her daughter ever learn to handle life with its ups and downs? Unfortunately, the die was already cast this time around. "Most of the time at your age, boys are mean to a girl when they like her," Diana teased, hoping to restore her daughter's natural happy place.

"Yuk," she said, scrunching up her face.

Diana chuckled. They slid out of the booth and moved to the register to pay the bill. She dropped a twenty and the tab on the counter, not looking for more conversation about Chad with anyone. "Keep the change," she said, moving off. "We need to stop by the dealership before we head back to the inn to pack. Mommy needs to take care of some unfinished business." She would have liked to cancel the deal on the truck as well. But with all the extra stuff they owned now, she would need the space.

"Okay. What's going to happen to Chad? I like him." Her daughter's question took Diana by surprise.

Diana wished she had an answer, but that wasn't the case. "I don't know, honey. Justice. I mean, if he committed the crime, he'll go to jail. We have to trust in God that if he's innocent, the truth will set him free." It was something she had included in her prayers last night and something she would continue to do until the truth came out.

Helping her daughter into the truck, Diana then climbed in the way Chad taught her, and started the engine. The sound didn't jazz her as much today, not with the weight of everything else on her plate. "Oh, and we need to run by the real estate office." She needed to sign some paperwork to officially cancel the contract on the dairy farm.

She pulled into a front row parking spot at the dealership. Hand in hand, they headed inside. "Hey, there. Back to finish the paperwork?" Victor asked when he spotted her.

Diana wobbled her head from side to side, her lips pursed. "Sort of. Can I talk to you for a minute?"

"Of course. I hope everything is okay with the truck?" he asked, his expression suddenly one of worry.

But then the idea of losing the sale would do that to someone. "It is. Lindsey and I are leaving town. With everything going on, it seems to be the right direction for us to take. That being said, I do need the truck as we've outgrown the car and I'm not sure I can trust it anymore."

Victor's relief was obvious. "So, what do you need from me?"

"A couple of things, actually. First, can you take care of either selling or junking my Buick? Whichever you think is best."

"I might know someone who's looking for a cheap car. I'll take care of it for you. What else?" he asked, eyeing her with interest.

"I need you to tear up the loan docs. I've decided to pay in cash." It no longer mattered if Diana kept her wealth a secret from the folks of Crossroads Creek since they were leaving town.

Victor's mouth dropped wide open. "But that's a lot of money. Close to fifty-five thousand with doc fees and taxes."

Diana nodded. They'd gone over all the details yesterday and she knew full well what the truck costs. "Money I can have transferred to your account within twenty minutes"

"*Ummm*, sure thing." Victor seemed as though he was about to have a meltdown, although why, Diana didn't have a clue.

Maybe it wasn't an everyday occurrence to have someone pay cash, but truly couldn't be a first for his business. "Cash is as good as a loan, right?"

"Absolutely. Let me get the paperwork changed to a cash sale. I'll be right back." Victor scurried off before she even answered.

Odd way to react, but none of her business.

Fifteen minutes passed, when Victor finally came out of the office.

Sirens filled the air, and suddenly the place was lit up like a blue-light special. "What's going on?" she asked, terrified there was a criminal on the loose and they had tracked him here.

Victor looked pale. "I...I...d...d...don't know," he mumbled.

Diana gripped Lindsey's hand tighter, pulling her close as she tried to see what was happening.

The sheriff and two police officers came barreling in the showroom. "Diana Langley, you're under arrest for armed bank robbery. Turn around and put your hands behind your back."

Diana paled, a sudden dizzying rush consuming her as she tried to breathe. Surely she hadn't heard them right.

Lindsey started to cry.

The sobbing sound spurred Diana into action. "What's going on?" she demanded. "I've done nothing wrong. I demand to know on what grounds you're charging me?" There was no way they were going to arrest her.

"You've been hanging around Chad, our number one suspect. Yesterday, you were taking out a loan for a truck. Today, you show up here ready to pay cash. Coincidence? I think not. Unless you have some other verifiable explanation, I suggest you do as I asked," the sheriff said, moving closer, handcuffs primed and ready.

For her.

Lindsey's crying became louder, her daughter clinging to her leg.

Panic welled in Diana's chest. If the sheriff arrested her, what would happen to Lindsey? This madness had to stop and at whatever cost. "I do have an explanation. It's called a trust fund. A verifiable source of money, I might add. And since I was here with Victor when the robbery occurred, you've got nothing on me. So quit trying to scare me and my daughter with your overzealous baboon tactics." She'd gone past shock and moved into anger.

The sheriff seemed a little off kilter. "Then why do all the paperwork for a loan? Why not just pay in cash in the first place?" he asked, his eyes narrowing to slits.

"I was trying not to draw attention to my finances. I've got a situation with an ex." Not to mention an entire lifetime of living under the microscopic inspection of people because her family had money, her parents and Silas being the worst.

The sheriff shook his head, but he did step back and give her some breathing room. "Sorry, you're not making any sense. And in light of everything going on, I'm going to need to know more of the details."

Diana nodded. "The money is in a trust fund my grandmother left me. My ex-husband is a gambler and I don't intend to let him get to the money, which meant staying off his radar. You can verify what you need to by calling my accountant. Here's the number," she said, digging in her purse to find the business card. Diana handed it to him.

"So why the sudden change in heart? Victor tells me you're leaving town," he asked.

Diana frowned at Victor, the man a little too generous with information. "Silas found me here anyway. He tried to blackmail me, but Chad convinced him to leave the farm. Silas headed back to New York City, but now, as for me and my daughter, I think it's time we moved on again. To stay one step ahead of him." A little too late, she remembered Lindsey was by her side and she sent her daughter an apologetic look.

"*Hmmpphh.* Wait here and watch her," the sheriff said to one of the officers standing nearby. He turned back to her. "You're not going anywhere until I talk to this person." The sheriff walked away, his doubting-Thomas expression firmly in place.

Diana kneeled down beside her daughter and pulled her close. "It's okay, sweetheart. The sheriff just needs to make a call so he knows mommy wasn't involved in the bank robbery."

Tears welled up in Lindsey's eyes. "But they took Chad to jail. Are you going to j...jail?" she asked, the terror on her face breaking Diana's heart.

Now more than ever, they couldn't leave town fast enough. This must have been how Chad felt, and if he was innocent like her, how much worse to be wrongly accused and no one to give you an alibi to keep you out of jail?

The sheriff approached, his demeanor much friendlier. "You're clear. Sorry to have troubled you and your daughter. I hope you understand and won't think too badly of us." It would seem humble pie was on the menu.

Diana could be forgiving. "I get it. You're just doing your job. Just like I'm doing my job to protect my daughter, which is why we're leaving town."

The sheriff shook his head. "But running isn't always the answer."

Minutes ago, he was trying to arrest her. Now he wanted to offer her fatherly advice. "Neither is trying to arrest people for crimes they didn't commit."

And by extension...she meant Chad.

Chapter Fifteen

♥

AFTER CATCHING UP ON the milking and the other chores that needed doing, Chad finally felt some of the tension lifting. His anger still simmered on low after having spent a night in the slammer, but out on the property, breathing in the fresh air, had a way of making him forget.

Sheriff Jones had jumped at the chance to lock Chad up. But it was the sheriff's father who had been killed in the armed robbery, so it's not like Chad could blame the man's animosity, even if it was misdirected.

Maybe that's why it took him this long to decide to leave town. Maybe deep down, he wanted to pay for his father's sin as a way to help himself recover from the shock of what happened. His sister could have taken care of herself after she turned eighteen, but Chad stuck around until she was married. Perhaps as much for himself as for her.

Roxanne had been a sister-on-the-spot last night, having the wherewithal to call in a neighbor for help with the milking. Chad wasn't sure how she managed to pull it off, but he was grateful to her and to the man's two sons who had come over to help. Riding out on the trail, he used the time to check the fence line, but more than anything it was the smell of Texas bluebonnets he sought to eliminate the stench of jail that clung to the back recesses of his brain.

The connection with the land was settling...almost peaceful. More so than he could remember before his arrest.

Chad's phone rang, the sound startling his mare. He quickly silenced it, regretting his earlier distraction and failure to do so before the ride. "What's up, Paul?" Chad asked, the realtor's name flashing up on the screen.

"Heard you had some difficulty yesterday."

News traveled fast, but Chad was sure this particular news would have been at lightning speed in hyper-drive. "You could say that. But it's all good now and I'm back at the farm. It'll be better when the sheriff finds the real culprit."

"I hear you. I know you're dealing with a lot right now, but I've got to add to your headaches. Diana Langley has pulled out of the contract."

Chad's heart raced as he absorbed the last comment. "What do you mean? Why would she do that? For that matter, *can she do that*?" Chad closed his eyes momentarily, trying to regain control of his emotions and keep his mare settled.

"Said she needed to leave town. I heard she had some trouble over at Victor's dealership. Seems you aren't the only one the sheriff decided to harass and charge for the robbery."

Chad reined in Duchess. "That's ludicrous. Why on earth would he want to arrest Diana?" *Unless, of course, it was because of her association with him.* He couldn't even begin to imagine the fear she would have felt, especially with Lindsey to consider. "Sheriff Jones has lost touch with reality. Whatever happened to binding real estate agreements?" He let out a deep breath, seeing but not appreciating, the beauty of the land in that moment.

"They are. Except there was a cancel clause. Diana will pay a ten percent fee to walk away. I'm sure you can use the money while we get the place back on the market. Hopefully, it's enough to last."

He hadn't read the contract, putting his trust in his lifelong friend, but this rubbed him the wrong way. Maybe if it had been purely a business deal, but it wasn't. This was Diana. "No."

"What do you mean?" Paul asked.

"I've made it this long, and I'll finish as I started...on my own. I don't want Diana's money. I'd rather her be happy and able to take care of Lindsey, and if this is what she wants, then it's all good." To take her money wouldn't be much different from Silas and he wouldn't stoop to that level.

"Wow. Are you serious? Do you even hear what you're saying?" Paul asked, his voice laced with incredulity.

Chad nodded, knowing it felt right. If anything, it made him feel better after such a horrible last twenty-four hours. "I'm serious, and yes, I do know what it means. If we find another buyer, great. If not, so be it. I'll put off going to the city. Maybe it's time to lease some of the land. There's always something." It was true. He had alternatives, it was just a matter of reconciling his heart with whatever the future held for him.

Paul let out a long, low whistle. "I know what the problem is. You like her, don't you? More specifically, did you do something stupid and like fall in love with the woman? This was supposed to be a business deal."

Love. An interesting word, even if it was way off. *Care.* Absolutely. Everything about Diana caught his attention, and he cared about her. It wasn't hard to admit because it was true. And it's not like he hadn't thought about kissing her, because he had. But love...that wasn't possible. "I'm not in love. I just want to do the right thing by her. She's had a rough go of it lately, and I'm not planning on adding to the list of people who take advantage of her."

"Fine, have it your way. But when you can't make ends meet, don't blame me. I tried to talk some sense into you," Paul said.

"You're off the hook, trust me." Chad hung up the phone. The problem was, his friend was right. It wasn't the best business decision, but Diana wasn't just a stranger on the other end of the contract. When she asked him to teach her how to run the farm, everything changed as they spent time together. And then there was the precocious Lindsey who looked up to him, much the same way his sister had done when she was that age. The feeling of doing something good for someone, helping...well, that was downright satisfying.

It still left him with the ranch and he was right back where he started from, but he'd deal with that the same way he always had. *One day at a time.* He reined Duchess to the left and headed for the fort. *His place of peace.* A place he hadn't been in years other than when he brought Lindsey and Diana here. Why he wanted to share a piece of his past with them, he hadn't been sure, but it was one more of the odd connections they'd shared that Chad couldn't seem to forget.

He dropped the reins. "Stay, girl." It was an unnecessary command, as Duchess was more than aware of what to do. Chad moved closer to the tree and tested the ladder rungs. *Solid.*

It was as though the place were calling to him...days long gone...but the memories were still there. Decision made, he started to climb, the pull inexplicable. It seemed a lot smaller than it once had as he hoisted himself through the opening. His gaze drifted to a couple of plastic bags from the local grocery store. *Not old and left behind.* New and with drink and snack trash. Vanilla wafers. Water. Kettle chips. Even spearmint gum.

A vague memory tickled his brain, but it eluded him. There were more important issues to deal with at the moment.

Someone else had found the fort and was using it. And by the looks of things, on a regular basis. In all the years he lived here, not once did they have trespassers dare to come this far onto the property? Not that it was like the Wild-Wild-West Days and anyone would get shot. But the law would be in on the action if someone dared to show their face a second time after being warned off.

Chad opened the last bag, one from the five and dime store in town. A scrunched-up plastic bag revealed someone had bought a pack of large T-shirts. Adult large. As in a man, not a boy. As if he didn't have enough problems to deal with already, it would seem there would be one more.

After collecting all the bags, his gaze drifted to the river. His favorite view. Again, a sense of peace came over him. At least, it did until he glanced down at the trash he held. Chad shook his head, mulling over a list of who might be foolish enough to squat on his property. And the very thought of some man out here when Diana might have lived here alone with Lindsey had him thinking doubly hard. Fear for their safety had him glad they weren't buying the place.

Maybe this was God's way of protecting them.

It didn't seem as though God had a hand in Chad's life...but Diana it would seem was a different story. Then again, it made sense. Her faith was strong even after all she'd been through, a testament to her character. It was Chad who fell short of the glory.

As he hung the bags from the saddle horn, he mounted up and headed for the house, and turned his thoughts to possible people stupid enough to trespass. Someone with a reason to hang out in the middle of nowhere.

A large T-shirt didn't rule out a lot of people, even in a town the size of Crossroads Creek. He thought back over the past weeks, and an image flashed in his head. *Silas*. What if he hadn't left town, and this had been his doing? His way to track her until the deal closed. Then he'd be on hand to wreak havoc on her life until she capitulated to the blackmail. The more he thought about it, the more it made sense. Chad urged his horse forward, intent on checking around the barn and house for more evidence that would point to Silas.

Chad led Duchess to the hitching post, letting her get a drink of water from the trough while he went into the barn. He scoured every corner just to be sure, one way or the other.

Ten minutes later, he was more than certain he had his answer. *Silas.* There was no one else who would be so brazen as to hang out in the barn. Chad picked up a shirt tucked under a bale of hay, a small corner hanging out. He moved the entire bale, only to find a pair of trousers, oddly similar to what Silas had worn when he first arrived, complete with three empty gum wrappers. Spearmint gum. The same gum Silas had been chewing when he paid Diana a visit, the memory of the gum wrapper on the ground finally coming back to him.

Of course, there was no proof, and without it, the sheriff wouldn't give Chad the time of day. Chad would keep searching, maybe even do some scouting around town tomorrow. The sheriff had asked him about enemies...and he had made one in Silas. A jealous ex-husband was no picnic for anyone involved, especially not the woman he was once married to. Correction, a jealous ex-husband willing to blackmail Diana for money. Fifty-thousand dollars. A man crazy enough to rob a bank and try to pin it on Chad.

The theory worked in his head, but not on paper. How would Silas know the details of his father's crime?

The internet.

Of course. Every last detail would have been reported over and over again, and failing that, he could have talked to someone in town. The perfect way to get to Diana and get rid of Chad. *And it might have worked.* That was the truly scary part.

With any luck, Silas wouldn't find out yet that Diana had backed out of the deal. Because with

Chad on his trail, the man might just slip up. But first he had to find him. It was high time luck started rolling in on his side. But just in case luck wouldn't do, Chad said a silent prayer. *Anything to protect Diana and Lindsey.*

Images of fire danced in Chad's head as he drifted in and out of sleep. He turned over for the umpteenth time that night, unable to get Silas and Diana out of his brain. The nightmare was so real, he could smell the smoke as it drifted on the night air.

Except odors weren't a part of dreaming. His eyes flew open, suddenly alert. The acrid smell of smoke rent the air and was as real as possible. He sprang to his feet and darted to the open window, dread piercing him as he spotted the source.

The barn was on fire.

Chad pulled on his boots, needing to get to the animals. Of course, his bad luck hadn't run out. It never did. Racing toward the barn, he put a call out to the fire department.

"This is Chad Thompson. My barn is on fire." He shoved the phone in his pocket, hoping they would get here fast. As he drew near, he spotted a figure running into the woods. Tempted to go after the man, he tamped down the urge, his animals far more important. This wasn't a case of bad luck, more than likely, a case of Silas strikes again.

Chad raced into the barn, leaving both doors open. He turned open all the stall doors to let the horses out, giving each a pat on the back flank to urge them to run free. Most of the cattle were out to pasture, but one by one, he led the few that weren't out into the dark night. It all took time, the smoke filling his lungs as he held a bandana over his mouth when possible. Sweat dripped down the sides of his face, the heat of the fire increasing. Soon, the barn would be a total loss, judging by the speed at which the place was going up in flames.

He chased a few chickens out the doors, hoping that once outside, they would all know well enough to avoid the burning building. Making one last run inside, he looked around, hoping all the kittens had made it outside as well. Not spotting any of them, he grabbed some of his tack gear, hoisting his saddle into his arms before running outside.

The sounds of the fire trucks racing down the driveway were reassuring. He met them out front. The paramedic took hold of his arm and led him to an ambulance.

"Let us take over," the fire chief said when Chad tried to pull away. "You need oxygen. Is there anyone else in the barn?"

"No. And the animals are all out. But I need to round them up."

"You need to do as I've asked. Some of the people from town will be here soon to help, I'm sure of that. You don't have to do everything alone, Chad."

"*Hmmpphh*. Not how I see it." Chad stopped resisting, knowing oxygen would clear his head quicker and then he could get back to work.

The chief seemed about to say something, but clearly changed his mind as he started to walk away. Stopping six feet away, he turned back. "One other thing. Any idea how the fire started?"

"I have a good idea." The people in town would probably assume Chad did it for the insurance money, but he'd never do anything of the sort. He wasn't a cheat, and he would never put the animals in jeopardy. "It's called arson. I saw a man running out the back when I arrived."

The chief nodded. "Gotcha. That will give us a good lead to run with when we open an investigation. Sorry this happened."

"So am I." Chad nodded, as the paramedic covered his face with an oxygen mask. At least the fire chief seemed prone to listen to his opinion and consider the possibility.

The sound of wood splitting as it fell to the ground had him spinning around to watch. The side wall collapsed as flames shot out from every window and door and through the roof where it had given way. There was no doubt in his mind about the arson, the fire taking hold far too quick. Whoever set the fire had used plenty of flammable materials and propellant to speed up the destruction. There'd be nothing left, not even with the massive amounts of water pouring through the hoses to put the fire out.

All too soon, it would turn into a controlled burn, not a save-the-barn effort. If this was Silas, and Chad was fairly certain it was, come morning, he'd be telling his suspicions to the sheriff whether he wanted to hear about them or not. More than likely, the man would accuse Chad of trying to cover his tracks, but at least he'd have another lead to follow up on.

Jealous ex-husbands capable of blackmail were capable of a whole lot more to get what they wanted.

Something Sheriff Jones couldn't ignore.

Chapter Sixteen

♥

CHAD WAS SURPRISED WHEN several people from town showed up to help round up the animals, checking to make sure they were all safe and accounted for. It would seem the fire chief had been right on that score. It was an eye opener, knowing not everyone hated him...well, hate was a strong word. Perhaps disliked with a grudge.

The ones who showed up treated him like...a neighbor. It was confusing at best, given all that he believed over the years, leaving him to wonder if his sister was right. Maybe living under a shell at the farm hadn't allowed him to move forward in life, just as perhaps keeping to himself allowed some of the people in town to continue the grudge. What if a lot of the reasons life had turned out the way it did, was because of his own fears? Or his own guilt in knowing it was his father who had sunk low enough to rob a bank...at gunpoint, no less, and killing the sheriff by accident. Not that it mattered...the decision to commit the crime had left a man dead, leaving his father one hundred percent responsible.

And then there was the fact he'd overheard his father talking to someone about money. A conversation he wished he could have unheard. It wasn't as though he'd garnered any details, but after the fact, it was clear his father had been planning the robbery with someone.

Someone who had never been caught. Chad had kept the information to himself, afraid he would be considered an accomplice. Something he couldn't risk...not when it would leave his sister alone and unprotected.

The acrid smell of smoke hung in the air, and Chad only managed a few passing moments of sleep through the wee hours of the morning. It was a smell that would take a long time to get out of his head. The fireman had soaked the barn rubble, making sure any lingering source of heat was extinguished.

As dawn broke, casting light through the window, Chad made a fresh pot of coffee. Fire or no fire, the cows had to be milked. And that's when it hit him like a punch to the solar plexus.

No barn. No milking equipment. No milk. No income. No nothing.

The cows were his priority. It would take long extra hours to hand milk them all, hours he didn't have. Chad knew what he had to do, although admitting defeat wasn't his forte. The cows needed to be relocated where they could get the proper care and milking.

He paced the kitchen, trying to figure out where to sell the rest of his herd, including Ruffian, his prized bull. With several farmers in mind, Chad started calling around some of the folks he knew in Fontana and Wylie. By eight, they were sold and being picked up mid-morning. One less thing for him to worry about.

Chad was relieved the cows would get milked this morning, even if a little late. A cow that didn't get milked regularly when they were in season would be uncomfortable and find it painful, much like a mother and a baby.

The clean-up process would take some time, and any chance to rebuild and start over would have to wait until the insurance company paid him. Something they wouldn't do without a thorough investigation, considering their first inclination would be insurance fraud. Everyone in town knew he was short on money. It also meant it was time to make the dreaded call to Fred Haskins, the rancher who had wanted to lease Chad's land for years. There was no other choice, but that call he'd put off a bit.

The hot coffee scalded the back of his throat, but at least he was pulling out of the tired fog that had settled in his brain.

After checking on the animals, he grabbed a rake out of the shed. Staring at the pile of black ash, he shook his head. This would take days, but then apparently, he had all the time in the world since Diana backed out of the contract. Which given the circumstances was also for the best, seeing as he didn't have a dairy farm to sell her anymore. Just land. Prime real estate, but that's all it was anymore.

Chad made a mental note to call the people in Dallas and cancel his rental contract, something else that would cost him quite a bit of money. He was under no illusions they would waive the fee the way he had with Diana. For them, it would be business as usual, while nothing about Diana fell under that category.

He wiped the sweat from his brow. The late morning sun was out in full force. The sound of a vehicle coming down the drive, along with the swirl of dust, alerted him to a visitor. It turned out to be two visitors, the O'Reilly boys who had helped with the milking the night he spent in jail, and then with the fire last night. They waved as he approached.

"Morning," John called out as he headed for the back of the truck.

"Morning," Randy hollered.

They were in good moods, given the circumstances. But then, they might not have had any trouble catching a few hours of sleep after the fire had been put out. For Chad, sleep had eluded him. "Good morning. Thanks again for your help with the animals. What's up?" he asked, confused when they unloaded rakes and chains.

John grinned. "Here to help. What else? Cleanup is never fun. Brought some chains so we could hook up to the tractor to haul off some of the bigger pieces. If we work together, might get this done by tomorrow. Dad said he'd get someone to cover our chores so we could help you out."

Chad was blown away by the generosity. "You don't have to do that." They didn't have to, but he couldn't honestly say it wouldn't be appreciated.

"We know," Randy quipped. "It's what neighbors do. Help one another out. Besides, gets us out of regular chores."

"I see. Well, I won't say no if that's what you were hoping," he said, still not used to this outpouring of neighborly kindness.

John grinned. "Not hoping that at all. Change of pace brings a fresh outlook on the monotony of everyday life and chores. Something we all need now and then to succeed in this life we've chosen." He chuckled.

"Well, okay then. Let's get to work." The truth in John's words landed hard. Chad did look at life on the farm as monotonous. Perhaps he wasn't the only one who felt trapped. But a change of pace? That wasn't something he'd ever tried or thought of. How did one change the pace of something so monotonous as dairy farming?

Diana.

The thought came out of nowhere. She changed the pace alright. Every day with her had been more fun, more relaxed, more...everything. It was as though she brought the sunshine and the bright light cast a glow over all that she touched. Her humor. Her smile. Her positive attitude. Especially in light of all she had been through. Chad could learn a lot from her playbook.

And here he thought he was the teacher. Instead, Diana had been teaching him how to live life and enjoy it. *Including the farm.*

"So, what are you going to do with the cows?" John asked.

"Sold them to Brighton over in Wylie. He's coming to get them this morning and will get them milked right away."

John nodded. "Sounds like a good plan. Figured you wouldn't have much choice. Shame though."

"Agreed, but perhaps for the best." At least, that's what Chad could hope for. Perhaps a new beginning was on the horizon for him in a way he hadn't foreseen.

"Hey, if you bring the tractor around, I'm going to hook up some of the bigger logs. Figure out where you want them," Randy said as he started to wrap the heavy chains in strategic places around the largest pieces of charred wood.

"Sure thing." Chad headed for the lean-to shed where he kept the tractor parked, grateful it started on the first try. It didn't always happen that way. Backing into position, he couldn't help but once again appreciate the help of these two men. There had to be a way to repay their kindness, as he didn't like owing anyone anything.

John hooked up the first board to the tractor. "Clear," he hollered, waving for Chad to move forward. The two men stepped back and out of the way. They did this over and over for the next few hours, clearing out the debris.

"We should stop for lunch soon. You can come on up to the house. I'm sure I've got something to make sandwiches," Chad said, handing them each a bottle of water.

"Another thirty minutes or so and we'll have this whole section done," John said, pointing to the back right section they'd been working on.

"Sounds good to me," Randy chimed in.

If they weren't ready to stop, neither was he. "Well then, I guess it's decided." Chad grabbed a rake and started to move the charred ashes to one pile at the side. Section by section, he cleared the debris. He wiped the sweat from his brow when it trickled into the corner of his eye, the stinging burn and blur forcing him to stop a second. A quick glance at the others, who showed no signs of stopping, and Chad started back in to work.

The rake caught and held. Moving it back and up at the same time, he tried to shake it free, but the debris had the tines firmly snagged. Chad stepped forward, manually pulling the tines from whatever held it, surprised to discover it was a cloth bag. Which made no sense since it was beneath where the floorboards had been laid out, and it had burned up into ashes in the fire. He kneeled down to take a closer look.

"What'd you find?" Randy asked, coming to stand next to him.

"No idea. There was a bag stashed under where the floorboards would have been." Chad wrestled it from the hole. It wasn't heavy by any means. He pulled his knife from his pocket and sliced the tie holding it closed.

Money fell out. "What the..." Chad exclaimed, looking up at the other two men. "I swear I have no idea where this came from," he said defensively. Finding a wad of money was a shock that rocked him to the core. *Unless...please, God, no.* The money his father stole was never recovered.

"Not bringing up old news, but there is the obvious," John said, suddenly sounding unsure of himself.

"You're probably right." Chad swallowed hard, the sick feeling in the pit of his stomach growing exponentially with each passing second. He picked up a stack of bills, seeing but not seeing.

Randy peered over his shoulder. "No, man. Not possible."

"What do you mean?" Chad asked, trying to wrap his head around the discovery.

"These bills were printed two years ago. Your old man robbed that bank ten years ago."

John clapped him on his shoulder. "He's right, Chad. This isn't your old man's. Besides, the bag looks new."

"True. What if it's from the bank robbery in town yesterday?" Randy asked, a pensive expression on his face.

The elephant in the room had just landed with a boom. They wanted to know if the sheriff was right and Chad had robbed the bank. It was a fair question. And beyond that, this was all the proof Sheriff Jones would need to have Chad locked back up in jail by the end of the day.

"Did you do it?" John asked, his voice low and quiet.

Chad shook his head. "No. But I've got a good idea who might have. All conjecture at this point, but it's all I've got to keep me out of prison."

"If it counts for anything, I believe you," John said, nodding.

"Why?" Chad asked, jerking his head up to gaze at John and see if he was telling the truth. It wasn't at all what he expected to hear.

John shrugged. "I saw the surprise on your face when you discovered the bag, and when you opened it. Not only that, but any man who also is willing to risk life and limb to save his animals doesn't have the heart to hurt others or pull off a crime of that nature. It takes someone with a blackheart, something you don't have."

Chad let out a sigh of relief. John's opinion might be one in a hundred. It was convincing the other ninety-nine that would be the problem. "Thanks. It does mean a lot. Too bad others won't see it the way you do." Chad hadn't done anything to deserve this kind of friendship, but right now, the man's friendship offering was like that of a life ring to keep him from drowning.

Randy nodded. "I agree with John, for what's it worth."

"Great. Three to one against a sheriff who hates me. Guess who wins?" Chad retorted.

"There is that," John admitted.

"Not that I blame him. My father killed his father, that's not something you forgive. Or forget," Chad voiced the thoughts he'd kept to himself all these years.

"I hear you, but it's not right to hold you responsible," Randy offered.

"Unfortunately, you know we need to call the sheriff," John said, the words seemingly pulled from him.

Calling was the right thing to do. "I'll do it," Chad said. He didn't want to involve the men any more than they were already. At least he had two eyewitnesses regarding the discovery. Besides, why would he hide the money in his barn and then burn it down? No one in their right mind would accuse him of both crimes and expect to convince a jury.

Within fifteen minutes, Sheriff Jones arrived, blue lights flashing. The man exited the patrol car and headed their way.

"Afternoon boys." The sheriff nodded as he approached.

"Sheriff," Chad said by way of greeting.

"Sorry to hear about your barn fire. I was out of town last night following up on some information I received on a case," the sheriff said, although not giving up details.

Chad had wondered about his absence. "Thanks. The guys are here to help me clean up." Chad stepped forward and handed Sheriff Jones the bag of money. "Eighteen thousand, three hundred and seventy-two dollars." He'd taken the time to count it, wanting to know how much he turned in and to make sure all of it was accounted for when it was admitted as evidence. His level of trust when it came to money was sorely lacking.

"Interesting number, as the estimated amount from the bank robbery in town is eighteen thousand." The sheriff glanced inside the bag. "Any thoughts of how it got here?" He eyed

Chad with curiosity, but at least he wasn't already pulling out the cuffs to haul him off to jail again.

Chad nodded. "One. At least one that makes sense."

"Let's hear it," Sheriff Jones said, his tone more than a little interested.

"This is a first." Chad couldn't help the resentment in his voice.

The sheriff frowned. "I'm asking, aren't I? Don't push your luck, son."

"Sheriff Jones, Chad was just as surprised as we were when he found it. Can't fake surprise that good." John was voluntarily coming to his defense, the man proving over and over he would be a true friend. If only Chad had given the O'Reilly boys the chance before now.

"I'll be the judge of that. So start talking," he said, turning to Chad.

"Truth is, I was going to call you later today anyway. I figured you'd want to know someone's been trespassing and hanging out around here. I've got an old fort on the back forty by the river. Just yesterday, I found some fresh plastic bags and trash there. I did some digging around and also found some clothes in the barn and some water bottles near the house perimeter. Someone's been scoping out this place who shouldn't be here. Add to that the barn fire and the loot...and it would seem to me, that everything might be connected." Telling the sheriff everything in front of the O'Reilly boys served a double purpose...witnesses to the information so the law wouldn't find it easy to discount the possibilities.

The sheriff nodded. "Might be. Any idea who would do this and want to set you up as the fall guy?" The man rubbed his lips as though chewing over the details.

"Silas Gibson," Chad said without hesitation.

The sheriff's eyes widened, as though he recognized the name. "Interesting."

"How so?" Chad asked, curious about the sheriff's reaction.

"It's not the first time I've heard the name. Came up yesterday when I was questioning Diana." He stopped short, as if realizing he was about to say too much.

"Silas is her ex-husband, and he came around here early last week. I sent him packing when he tried to extort money from her using the custody of her daughter as blackmail." Chad had promised Diana not to tell others about what happened, but the fact the sheriff knew meant Diana herself had disclosed the information and Chad didn't feel the need to maintain secrecy any longer. This was about catching a criminal that might be far more guilty of crimes that went beyond blackmail. The man deserved to be behind bars if what Chad suspected was true.

"So she told me. We've been doing some checking into his background. I need to make a phone call. Don't go anywhere."

"Of course not." Chad frowned.

The sheriff moved off, talking on his phone.

"Wow. Interesting turn of events. This might end well after all," John said with a grin.

"One can hope," Chad said, more than ready for a change in his luck.

The sheriff shot them a quick look, before shoving his phone in his back pocket. He approached, still tightly clutching the money bag. "Any idea where I can find this Silas Gibson guy for questioning?"

"Wish I did. I planned to start poking around and checking into things on my own. At least I was until the barn burned down. My thoughts are that Silas was waiting for the sale on the farm to finalize, and for me to leave town. Then he'd come in and start harassing Diana. Only he was making sure I went out in style. Figure the poor schmuck was playing the jealous ex-husband role a little too jaded, seeing as Diana and I are friends. Guess he didn't believe us."

At least that was the same story he would tell anyone who wanted to know. The truth went much deeper for him, but with so much going on, Chad hadn't had any time to really think through and understand his true feeling for Diana.

"Let me know if you see or hear anything. But I'm a little worried about what the man might do when he finds out he's a person of interest in burning the barn, armed robbery, and in black-mail. The two of you need to be extra careful, and then there's the little girl to consider."

Chad felt as though several dark shades of life had been lifted, and that maybe his life was about to change for the good. "True. Maybe you can have someone to keep an eye on Diana and her daughter until this is resolved."

"Sounds like a good idea."

"So you believe me? About Silas...and everything?" Chad asked, relieved the sheriff's animosity had lessened, but needing to hear the words.

"I do," the sheriff said, his voice solemn.

"Why now?" Chad asked.

"Two reasons really. For one thing, this bag," the sheriff held it up, "is a fireproof bag. I called the hardware store in Crossroads Creek, and then in Fontana and Wylie, as they are the closest towns. Turns out a bag like this was purchased two nights ago...at the same time you were sitting in a jail cell." The sheriff shook his head. "I want to apologize for jumping the gun on arresting you. I do have some resentment, but clearly it's misguided. Although, perhaps in this case, you could see your way to forgive me, as I did manage to give you an alibi. I love the law, but I let my personal emotions get in the way of the truth, something I won't let happen again."

Chad stilled. It was like a mountain had been lifted from his shoulders. "I'm glad to hear your change of heart. It's an odd thing to be thanking a man for, throwing him in jail...but thank you." Perhaps blessings came in a great many disguises. A night in a jail cell in exchange for his freedom and perhaps to a new life. One that looked like his old life, but with things changed up a bit. His thoughts drifted to Diana. She'd canceled the contract because of him, but now pieces were falling into place that would make leaving unnecessary.

"Can they identify Silas from the charge card?" Chad asked.

The sheriff shook his head. "Unfortunately, he paid cash. But I've got some other officers questioning local businesses to see if anyone else saw him and checking for video footage. We've got his picture, although the clerk can't positively

ID the man as she was really busy trying to close the store when he checked out."

"I see. That does stink. You said there were two reasons. What's the other?" Chad asked, recalling the sheriff's earlier comment.

"Seems some folks in town saw you sitting on your sister's porch. Their stories all seem to check out, placing you and your phone at her place."

Chad grinned. "Well, I'll be darned. On top of a night in jail, the nosey neighbors turned out to be a blessing. Add to that...helpful neighbors, and I'm triply blessed," he said, nodding at Randy and John.

The sheriff nodded.

"Any chance you could put in a good word for me with the fire investigators? It'd be good if I could get them to push through the claim. Can't build a new barn till it happens," Chad asked.

"I reckon I could do that. Seeing as I probably owe you one for the night you spent in a cell." It would seem the sheriff's attitude was changing.

Diana was in shock when news of the fire at the Thompson farm made its way around the breakfast table at the inn. There was no way Chad had anything to do with it, and in her heart, she knew he had nothing to do with the robbery. Determined to set things right with him, she headed over to his place after lunch, hoping to have a chance to talk before Lindsey got out of school.

She pulled into the driveway, surprised to find the sheriff there. The last time she had been here, it had been to watch Chad hauled off in handcuffs. *Please, Lord, not again.* Diana cared about Chad, more than she wanted to admit. And it was why this time, she wouldn't turn tail and run. She had to see him and let him know she believed in him. Something Diana should have done in the first place instead of believing what she heard and running away.

Chad looked up as she approached, but he didn't say a word. She couldn't blame him.

"Hey, there. I'm so sorry to hear about the fire. Are all the animals okay?" she asked.

"They are. Thanks for caring enough to stop by," Chad said, his intense gaze never leaving her face.

"Do you know what happened?" Diana asked, almost afraid of the answer. The minute she heard about the fire, a thought had taken hold...one she hadn't been able to shake.

"It would seem the barn was set fire by the same person who robbed the bank," the sheriff said, answering for Chad.

The sheriff wanted to blame Chad for the robbery, but this was over the top. "But why? I don't understand," she cried out, moving closer to Chad in a show of support.

"To eliminate evidence and throw us off the scent. Almost worked, until Chad uncovered the money," the sheriff added.

Shock rifled through Diana. "Wait, what? Chad found the money from the bank robbery?" Now she was more confused than ever as she glanced between the two men, trying to figure it all out.

"That's what I'm trying to tell you. It would seem the bank robber was trying to frame Chad at the same time." The sheriff silenced the radio strapped to his hip.

"But who?" she asked, knowing the answer deep in her heart. For Lindsey's sake, she prayed it wasn't true.

"Silas," Chad said, the one-word bomb exploding in the air.

Diana sucked in a deep breath. It was as much as she suspected but prayed wasn't true. "I'm so sorry," she said. She was the one who brought all of the troubles Chad was facing to his doorstep. He had almost gone to jail because of her.

"It's not your fault. The man's desperate for money. And jealousy is a strong motive to wipe out the competition. Silas would obtain both goals with the plan he put in motion. He's still only a suspect, but we have enough to pick him up on," the sheriff said, filling in details.

"Jealous? That part is not true, I'm sure. Silas has only ever loved himself."

"Sometimes it's losing what you have and seeing that person has moved on that can trip the way a person reacts. He didn't like seeing you here...with me. He made no bones about that fact."

Except there wasn't anything between her and Chad for Silas to see...was there? Or at least not that Diana was aware of when it came to Chad having feelings for her. As to her own feelings, she hadn't told a soul. "I still find it hard to believe, but this morning, it did cross my mind. Do you have evidence? Because if you don't it will never stick. His family will hire the best attorneys and there's nothing you can do to beat them. And he'll never stop coming after me until he wins. Anything to protect his reputation from being sullied." She was sick to her stomach to think she'd brought all this to Chad's doorstep.

"Not hard evidence, but we're working on it," the sheriff said, telling her the truth. The sheriff's phone rang, and the man stepped away to answer.

A dizzy spell washed over her. The truth of the situation was overwhelming. "I'm so sorry, Chad. I should have never come here." She put a hand on his arm to steady herself. "I'll be leaving town soon as soon as the sheriff gives me the go ahead."

"But why do you have to leave? I know you didn't trust me, but now you know the truth. We can go back to the way things were." Chad grabbed the hand on his arm and pulled her closer, gazing deeply into her eyes.

More ashamed than ever, Diana looked away, unable to bear the truth. "You're right, I didn't trust you, at least not when I saw you being hauled off in handcuffs. I should have trusted my instincts and had more faith in you. You're a better man than I gave you credit for, Chad Thompson. You need to step up and take charge of your life. And it's here, you know, the dairy farm. It's you through and through, and you'll never be happy if you leave it."

Chad turned her face toward his, his soft touch gentle against her chin. "You might be right," he said, taking her by surprise, and brushing a lock of hair off her cheek. "But the place looks a lot better with you in it."

Diana stepped back, torn between his words and the possibilities they formed in her head. Chad cared, but it was too late for her. "I can't stay. We can't stay. Silas. This won't end. It will only get worse, and I've done enough to destroy your life. We've got to leave. I should be gone by this weekend and your life will return to normal—but better."

"That can only happen with you in it," Chad said, his voice vibrating with a wealth of emotion.

"I'm sorry," Diana said, pulling away, tears falling down her face as she ran toward the truck. Leaving this time would be far harder than it had been to leave Silas and their marriage. And the reason, she finally understood, was because she'd fallen in love with Chad.

Chapter Seventeen

♥

THE PAST FEW DAYS brought Diana no joy. And Lindsey, having picked up on her reluctance to leave Crossroads Creek, played the dissatisfaction card to the max. Every day held a replay of the fun she'd had with her friends at school, or how much she loved her teachers, or even how much she learned that day. The list went on and on, especially when the subject of the horses and farm animals came up.

The sheriff hadn't found out anything new. He also no longer had a reason to keep Diana in town. It would seem Silas would get away with what he did unless some of the leads they were following turned up more information. Even

Allison hadn't been able to find anyone willing to talk about Silas and his whereabouts.

The truck was loaded, the process taking twice as long as necessary just because Diana was dragging her feet. She loved the farm, was fairly certain she was in love with Chad, and finally felt like she was fitting in somewhere she could belong. The fact that it was Silas who would destroy everything she had started to rebuild, only made it worse.

Diana checked her watch. It was time to pick up Lindsey after her last day of school. Janice had been kind enough to send her daughter to school with three dozen cupcakes for a farewell party, even letting Lindsey help make them the night before. Not that it had lifted Lindsey's spirits, but it was the kindness that counted. The same kindness Diana was loath to walk away from.

Sitting in the pickup line in front of the school, she was tempted to call Allison again. But personal calls weren't allowed, and too many trips to the ladies' room might be noticed by the ever-watchful eyes all around *Illusions Electronics*. Diana flipped on a country music channel, hoping to soothe some of the tension away. Except the song that was playing was more than a little heartbreaking, as it reminded her of Chad.

"*Alabama's* lyrics to the song *High Cotton* nailed the hardships of country life, but it also pointed out the rewarding aspects. It would seem Chad would get a chance to discover the rewards, which was exactly what he needed. More proof Diana was doing the right thing by leaving.

The school bell rang, Diana almost missing it, lost in her thoughts. Children started to appear through the double doors. Smiling, happy, laughing children.

Diana's phone lit up, Allison's name flashing across the screen. She pulled the phone from the dash mount. "Hey, there. What's up? I was just going to call you for an update, but didn't want to get you in trouble."

"Thank goodness you answered. I can't talk long. I came outside for a quick break. I'm grabbing a latte at the Corner Coffee cart," Allison said, her voice barely above a whisper.

"What's going on?" Diana asked, watching as Lindsey stopped to hug a teacher. The embrace was more like a tearful goodbye, the sight gut wrenching.

"Well, Missy Lumberton down in supply got fired this morning. I called her to see what happened, and she was a complete wreck. They claimed she took supplies home and fired her on the spot. She's a single mom and relies on her salary as their sole income."

"So did she? Take the supplies, I mean?" Diana asked, trying to understand why this was important enough for an emergency call, even though it definitely qualified as troublesome.

"Missy claims she didn't, and I believe her. It took some prodding, but she finally owned up to the fact that she had made the mistake of going out with Silas. And when she rejected his advances to take the date back to his bedroom, things got ugly. Next thing you know, she's got a pink slip from *Illusion Electronics*. Too convenient if you ask me."

At least Missy had the good sense to say no, for that Diana was thankful. The wreck Silas left in his wake could be so much worse. "I agree. Poor woman. His delicate ego seems to have taken a turn for the worse since the divorce." *Served the man right.*

"It gets better. When I told her he had tried to do the same to me, not the firing part as it was years ago, Missy seemed to feel better."

Years ago, but still after she and Silas were married. It was Allison who alerted Diana to the truth about Silas. "Connections can be found in the strangest of ways."

"There's more. Missy heard I'd been asking if anyone knew how to get in touch with Silas or where he was, and it turns out, our new bonding moment led Missy to want to tell me what she knew."

Diana kicked into full alert mode, suddenly understanding the importance of the call. "That's fantastic. Where is he?" Diana asked, as her daughter drew near. This wasn't a conversation for Lindsey to hear and she took it off speakerphone.

"Missy said Silas had sent her a couple of text messages that mentioned a trip to Texas and that he would deal with her when he got back into town. Silas turned up at the office this morning, and suddenly Missy was fired. So there you have it."

"Texas, huh? We knew he was here, but he'd planned to return to the city over a week ago." *Jealous ex-husband.* Chad's words rang in Diana's head, and it would seem he had a valid point. Nothing else made sense.

"At least it's proof he was in the state at the time of the robbery and the fire," Allison said.

Diana had brought enough trouble to Chad's doorstep, and she hated the thought of anything landing on her best friend's doorstep. "Be careful, Allison, or you'll be on the chopping block next. Silas isn't playing nice and apparently is willing to go to great lengths to keep his superior image of himself and the façade of a *golden boy* to others. Something that won't last long if he's arrested."

"I'm thinking of leaving, anyway. Without you around, I'm tired of the ridiculous demands made by my boss. I'd want a job where I'm respected for what I bring to the table, and where I actually like who I'm working for. Something that will never happen here."

"I'm sorry. You know I had to leave," Diana said, regretting that she'd left Allison to face off with others in her absence.

"I do know, and I'm proud of you for standing up and taking charge of your life."

"Thank you. Sorry, but I've got to run. Lindsey's out of school and about to get in the truck. I'll keep you posted to let you know where we end up moving."

"Stay safe. Silas can still make trouble for you, even if he's back in the city," Allison warned.

They both understood his character far too well. Unfortunately, neither had seen the real Silas until Diana had married the jerk. "I will. Bye."

Diana pressed the end button to hang up the call just as Lindsey tossed her bookbag in the back seat. She slid out of the truck, going around to the passenger side to help her daughter up into her booster seat. "How was your day, honey?"

"Not good since we're leaving." Lindsey's chin jutted upward in defiance.

"I'm sorry. If there were any other way...you know I'd choose to stay," Diana said, her heart breaking at the rift between them.

"Can we stop and see Chad before we go?" Lindsey asked, the question coming at her unexpectedly.

There wasn't anything she wouldn't do to make Lindsey happy at the moment, even if it would make leaving harder on Diana. "Of course."

She drove the short distance to the farm, surprised to see the sheriff's patrol car parked in front. Adrenaline shot through her body in warm flashes, the sight enough to make her panic. It would seem the trepidation of the sheriff's presence wasn't something that would go away, not since he arrested Chad. She'd always feared and respected law officers, but now there was an added edge.

Chad and the sheriff were on the porch, the pair stopping to turn and watch as she and Lindsey approached.

Lindsey broke away and raced ahead to greet Chad, hugging his leg. "I don't want to go," she cried. "I'll miss you and Dawning Light."

Chad kneeled down beside her. "I wish you didn't have to go either, pumpkin, but your mommy knows best. Trust her."

"But…"

"No buts. Trust your mom. She's smart, level-headed, and has your best interests at heart."

"Yes, sir," Lindsey mumbled.

Leave it to Chad to know just the right thing to say. Diana appreciated him coming to her defense, as his opinion would go a long way with her daughter.

"Can I go say goodbye to my horse, Mommy?"

"Of course. Just don't open the stall doors and come back in five minutes." Chad had ordered temporary stalls for the horses, even going so far as to build a lean-to that covered them in the interim while he waited for the insurance money to clear to build a new barn. The man was one of the most considerate people she knew, his care and concern extending to all the animals. Even the kittens had become indoor kittens living at the bunkhouse. Chad thought of everything.

"Okay," Lindsey said, moving off in the direction of the temporary stalls. It's not like she could tell time, but her daughter understood minutes was a short amount of time, and that's all that mattered.

"What brings you this way?" Chad asked.

"We just wanted to stop in and say goodbye." It was Lindsey's request, but the truth was, Diana seconded the notion. "And I didn't know you were here, Sheriff Jones, but seeing as you are, it will make it easier to tell you about something I heard."

"I'm glad you stopped in," Chad said simply, although it looked like he had more to say.

"What's up, Diana?" the sheriff asked.

"I know you're looking for proof about Silas, trying to connect the dots and tie him to the crime. I have access to proof that he was in Texas when the bank robbery and the fire happened if that would help. A friend of mine has access to text messages he sent to someone. More like sent with threats. Apparently, the Don Juan of the company has been getting more rejections than he likes lately."

The sheriff nodded. "Interesting. And yes, the more proof, the better."

"What do you mean, more proof?" Diana asked.

"I was just telling Chad that we got the judge to sign off a warrant to obtain Silas's phone records. We were checking phone tower pings and we can put Silas in Crossroads Creek and in Wylie. But the best news was that the dry cleaner across the street has a camera out front and they captured Silas coming out of the hardware store at the time of the fireproof bag purchase. I'd say we have enough to arrest his sorry backside for both the armed bank robbery and the arson. Not to mention blackmail, if you're willing to file charges against him."

The rush of emotion sent a tingling zipping through her body, her heart racing at the overwhelming news. Tears welled in her eyes. Silas wasn't going to be able to hurt them anymore. *They were free.* "His family will go crazy. They have some high-powered attorneys on retention," Diana said, still afraid to believe it would all work out.

"The difference is we have facts, and they will be going off fiction. The jury will see right through it," the sheriff added.

The sheriff truly believed Silas was going to prison, and for a very long time, based on the charges. Diana couldn't believe it. Maybe Missy could even get her job back. It was too late for Diana and Lindsey, but then, the truth was, she was happier here than she'd ever been. And now they didn't have to leave. It was as though a huge weight had been lifted off her shoulders, and Lindsey didn't have to be uprooted.

Except she'd let go of the contract on the farm and it wouldn't be their home. They'd find another place, she was sure. It just wouldn't be the place where her heart belonged.

"Such good news. I can't believe it. I'll think about the blackmail charges. I do have to think of Lindsey and the impact something like that would have on her going forward as it is still her father. Thank you for everything, Sheriff Jones."

"My pleasure. Sorry it all happened, and I do understand about thinking it over. It's not a pretty story."

"Thank you. *Ummm*...Chad, can I speak with you privately for a minute?" Diana asked, needing to know where he stood...on a lot of things. Silas's arrest changed everything for her, but did it change anything for Chad? That's what Diana needed to find out the most.

"Sure thing," Chad said, following her down the steps and off to the side of the house. "What's up?"

Diana rocked on the side of one foot and stared at the ground. "The thing is, with Silas out of the picture, there's no reason for Lindsey and me to leave Crossroads Creek. Any chance you're still willing to sell me the farm?" It was a long shot, but one worth taking.

Chad ran a hand through his hair and let out a deep breath. "Maybe."

Not exactly the answer she was hoping for...but she wasn't sure why.

The turnabout in events took Chad by surprise. He had previously thought that he would like to stick around town and perhaps the two of them would spend time together to explore the connection they shared. Today, she wanted to reinstate the contract on the farm, which would mean Chad would have to leave town as originally planned.

Except for two problems...one, it was no longer a dairy farm. Two, and still yet a bigger problem...Chad didn't want to sell the farm anymore.

Once upon a time, he thought Diana was on a fool's errand buying the place, but now he knew how wrong he had been. She belonged here, almost as much as he did. And he loved her. Enough to want her to be happy. "I'm sure we could work it out, but things have changed. I lost the milking equipment in the fire and had to sell the cows. A one-man operation couldn't keep up. The other thing is, I'm not sure I'll be headed to the city. I've reconsidered about some things and believe a change of pace will do me good, time to pursue new interests in my life. I can have Paul draw up the contracts, if you still want the land, that is?" Chad said, knowing deep down it was the only answer he could give. Diana and Lindsey's happiness were important to him.

"Really? Thank you so much," she said, throwing her arms around his neck and kissing him. A happy, friendly kiss, but talk about a nice surprise.

Chad was loath to release her...but he did. She fit perfectly with him in so many ways. All along it would seem, the answer had been that he needed the right woman by his side, a best friend with which to share life. Not skip through the parts and pieces he didn't like without trying to find some enjoyment.

"Really," he said, stepping back before he gave into the urge to kiss her...for real. A kiss that wouldn't be born of gratitude, but of love. With Diana, it was all possible, and Lindsey was a beautiful bonus. They were the missing piece to the farm that he always wanted but didn't think he could have. Someone to share the joys and heartaches that came with living life. Except sometimes, love meant letting someone go.

"I'm truly sorry about what happened with Silas. If I had trusted my heart, and not let my own past jade the truth, things could have been different. And it could be that way for you if you let it happen," Diana said, her closeness wreaking havoc with his brain.

"It's not that easy." Chad wanted it to be different—with Diana in the picture, but he truly doubted that's what she intended.

"Sure it is. And how's this for starters? I'll still buy the farm, but with one condition," she said, a coy smile on her face that gave him pause.

"Another condition? Let me guess...with the condition I stay another thirty days and help do what? Rebuild the barn? It's probably the least I could do." Chad grinned. Thirty days would give him time to convince her of how much he cared...a definite upside.

Diana shook her head. "You are a part of the deal, but I don't need thirty days to learn what I already know."

His heart sank to his toes. "And what's that?" he asked, wondering where all this was going.

"That I'd be a fool to let you slip away. My condition is that you stick around—indefinitely."

Chad must have heard Diana wrong. "That sounded remotely like a backhanded marriage proposal. Was it one?"

Diana grinned. "No. But it might be an invitation to forever down the road, if you play your cards right, cowboy."

Chad's heart soared as he picked Diana up and spun her around. "The answer is yes. Setting her down, he drew her close. "I agree to your condition but know this...I'm not a gambler. I consider this a sure thing because I'm already in love with you."

Diana wrapped her arms around his neck. "Well then, that's good. One gambler in my life was too much, but someone who loves me...now that I'm on board with. Especially considering

I happen to have it on good authority that I'm in love with a certain cowboy as well."

"You are?" he asked, not wanting to miss a heartbeat of the moment. This was truly a day the Lord had made, one that filled him with excitement and peace all at the same time.

"I am," Diana answered, her eyes brimming over with happy tears.

"I love those words," he murmured, leaning down to kiss her. Soft and gentle. *A kiss born of love, hope, and a promise of the future to come.*

Chapter Eighteen

♥

THE NEXT THREE WEEKS were spent with Diana working on the farm side by side with Chad. Nights were spent at the Serendipity. Time seemed to fly. Both she and Chad had agreed to hold off on selling her the land for a multitude of reasons, including the developing relationship between them that grew stronger with each passing day.

It was as though once they committed to take the step...the walls of insecurity came tumbling down. And with it, the ability for love to shatter any lingering doubts. There were decisions to be made, but they would be made together. Decisions that would affect their future.

Between painting the house and bunkhouse, fixing them up and making repairs, and checking fences, they had plenty to do. Adding in daily horseback rides together in the mornings, as well as rides with Lindsey afterschool, and it was a most idyllic time filled with hard work and laughter. The bond between the three of them grew stronger with each passing day.

The best news had been when the sheriff stopped by to inform them that Silas had been arrested and was denied bail as a flight risk. Even his high-dollar family team of attorneys hadn't been able to change the outcome. *Proof money couldn't buy everything.*

Diana had even reconciled with her parents for Lindsey's sake, and in the process had found peace for her own heart.

Lindsey barreled into the living room. "Are we leaving yet?" she asked for the third time in fifteen minutes. But then, Lindsey's excitement had been bubbling over on warp-five speed ever since she found out they weren't leaving town.

The local church had an excellent kid's program and her daughter had made more friends, and this morning Lindsey was more than ready to attend church.

"Yes, sweetheart. I'm ready." For Diana, however, this was more than just your normal Sunday at church. That is, if she didn't lose the nerve to make her announcement. It was time to bring the past to a close and bring in the future. Hers. Lindsey's. And Chad's.

Diana helped her daughter into the back seat of the truck. She'd gone over and over in her head what to say. It would require a delicate balancing act so as not to step on any toes, and the last thing she wanted to do was alienate folks.

She parked the truck and dropped Lindsey off at her youth room. "Have fun," Diana said, kissing the top of her daughter's head before shuffling off toward the sanctuary. Sitting more to the back of the room, she figured it would give her a chance to see who was in attendance.

The place was packed, everyone looking their best for Sunday. Everything from dresses and suits to jeans and cotton short-sleeve shirts, and everything in between. *The Sunday polish.*

The music started, the soft chords of the piano soothing. Some people sang, some people didn't, but they all stood to show their love for the Lord. The pastor's message hinted at forgiveness, perhaps at a different level, but forgiveness just the same. Which primed her request perfectly, so by the time it came for announcements, Diana was more than ready, empowered by God to her way of thinking.

The pastor closed out with a prayer. "Any announcements this morning to share?" he called out from the pulpit.

Diana searched the crowd, willing someone else to start. She swallowed hard, then stood, when no one else jumped in. "I do."

Everyone turned to face her, curiosity written in their gazes.

"Wonderful. Go ahead," Pastor Phil said, gesturing for her to begin.

Diana took a deep breath, her hands clenching the pew in front of her. "As you all know, forgiveness is key. Pastor Phil's message wasn't at my request, but perhaps God laid it on his heart for a reason. One key point is that forgiveness can heal your own hearts, not necessarily the other person's heart. We are only in control of our own hearts, so forgiveness, ultimately, is for ourselves.

"A long time ago, Jim Thompson committed a felony in this beloved town. He traumatized a lot of people and caused one family great sorrow. The whole town lost a well-loved and respected member of the community, and the pain and grief hasn't lessened. Holding on to this pain has shed negative feelings toward the rest of the Thompson family. Children innocent of any crime. I challenge you to forgive

Jim, not for his sake, but for your own. It's time to let go, so you can heal. And for those of you who still blame Chad and Roxanne for their father's shortcomings, it's time to recognize they are a part of this community, a good part."

There were a lot of nodding heads and some murmurs of agreement that gave her the courage to continue. "A few weeks ago, Chad's barn was burned to the ground. With the help of a few special neighbors, the place was cleared the following day, which led to some key evidence that helped the sheriff solve the recent armed robbery. It's a case of bad things happening for the greater good." A lesson Diana had to learn and embrace herself.

"The lumber to rebuild will be delivered Friday and the general plan is to start work on Saturday morning. That's my announcement...but here's my request and prayer. That you all forgive the wrongs of the past and show your change of heart by helping a member of the community who could use some kindness and an outpouring of love. Come by Saturday morning and join us for a barn raising event like none this town has ever seen. Let's show Chad just how welcome he is in the community. There'll be plenty of food donated by Janice Edwin, so you know the food will be good," she said, grinning at her friend, who sat with her husband one row up.

The buzz of conversation rose in the room.

"I second the request," Pastor Phil said, showing his support, in case there were any holdouts.

"I'm not asking you to commit this second. I'm asking that you pray about it privately, and if you can find it in your heart to move forward, please let Randy or John O'Reilly know you'll be joining us. That will give me a head count for the food preparation. Thank you all so much for hearing me out." Diana sat back down, twisting and turning her hands together as she glanced around the room.

She'd know soon enough how well received her request was, but for now, she'd simply continue to pray. For Chad. He was a good man and deserved happiness.

And Diana planned to be right there sharing it with him. She had been sure she loved him when she agreed to stay, but all doubts had been lifted over the last few weeks. Chad's true character was like a radiant gift of all she'd ever wanted in a husband. A man whose patience, understanding, and genuine kindness washed over her like the rays of the sun, enveloping her and Lindsey in its warmth.

Life certainly had a way of changing someone's outlook, and Chad was grateful it had happened to him in time. At peace with the farm and knowing he was planning to stay changed his outlook. He knew it was mostly due to Diana and Lindsey, but he had a renewed passion to make the place a success. Whether he went all in as a dairy farmer, or switched to a cattle ranch, he wasn't sure.

God had helped him to see what was important, and the joys in his life just kept growing. The O'Reilly's and a few others from town had reached out when he needed them, proof things were changing in Crossroads Creek.

And it was Randy and John who would be there this morning to help him tackle rebuilding the barn. It would take weeks, but the barn was almost symbolic of how he felt. Like the past was gone and a new life was just beginning. Several times he'd thought of asking Diana to marry him, but the timing wasn't right. He wanted it to be special. *Memorable*. Making memories with her and Lindsey brought him a deep-seated peace he found hard to describe.

Chad finished off a cup of coffee, filled the thermos, and headed out to the barn area to get started. The light of dawn was just beginning to filter over the countryside. One by one, he moved the boards into different areas by size and for the ease of handling. Organization was key to this project. He hadn't been at it long before Randy and John showed up. "Morning," Chad said, noting they were far more awake and alert than he was at the moment.

"Morning," they said in unison. "Great day to build a barn. Clear and crisp. Where do you want to start?" John asked.

Energy on caffeine or a natural high, Chad didn't know, but he was more than grateful for their help. "I've hauled some of the floor timbers closer and started to lay some of them out on the concrete for the floor framing. Check the plans I drew up and you could start cutting them to size."

"What an exciting day," John said, moving over to the saw to plug it in and check over the settings.

Chad shook his head. "Not sure how you two always seem to have such a positive outlook, especially when it comes to manual labor. I reckon I need it to rub off on me." He chuckled.

"Guess I figure what's the use of a negative outlook. Doesn't change the result, so might as well embrace what you're doing. Maybe it'll go faster." John grinned, shooting his brother a wink.

It was as if they had their own secret joke on the subject. Perhaps a brother thing, two people in sync with one another. "Interesting concept."

"You should try it." Randy chuckled.

Side by side, they took turns, hammering, cutting, measuring. Working together as a team, Chad was satisfied when he stepped back to see the work. It was slow going but happening.

An hour passed before Diana showed up with Lindsey, Roxanne right behind her. The two had become fast friends over the weeks, and Lindsey adored his sister.

"Good morning. You guys are doing great," Diana said, hugging Chad briefly, a shy smile on her face.

"Thanks. I wasn't expecting you here this soon, but it's a nice surprise," Chad said, his day always looking brighter when Diana showed up.

"One of many," she quipped, glancing over at Randy and John, a silent look passing between them all.

The same look the two brothers shared earlier. Something was up, and there was no telling what it might be if Diana was involved. The woman was as take-charge as anyone he'd ever met. "Oh, I like surprises. What is it?" Chad asked.

"Can I tell him?" Lindsey chimed in, her face glowing with excitement.

"No!" Both Diana and Roxanne had rushed to answer, making him even more curious.

There was definitely something afoot. "How about a little hint?" he asked, getting into the fun.

John and Randy came to stand next to the group.

"Morning, ladies," John said, nodding his head in their direction. "Reckon you'll find out soon enough," he said, shooting a grin at Chad.

The sound of a diesel truck coming down the driveway caught Chad's attention, the dust swirling in the air. And then there was another truck behind it. And another. And another.

What on earth was going on? One by one, they pulled up in front of the house. He recognized Pastor Phil at once, the man's royal blue Ford 350 quad cab, hard to miss.

"Diana?" he asked, searching for answers as about twenty vehicles parked in a line down his driveway. As people got out, he recognized them from town. Jerry. Alfred. Tommy. The list went on. They gathered in a group and headed his way.

"Heard there's a barn raising going on. Reckon you could use some help, Chad?" Jerry asked, reaching out to shake hands.

Chad swallowed hard and glanced back at Diana, and then at the others. They all knew. "*Ummm*, of course. I just don't understand," he answered, shaking the man's hand with a firm grip.

Jerry grinned. "Well, your lady friend did some rather fine explaining and asked for our help. We decided it was the right thing to do for a member of our community."

"A mem—"

"Explaining is an understatement," someone from the back of the crowd called out.

The group of men all laughed.

"Diana, Janice told Mary to tell me that she and the other women would be here in about an hour to start bringing in the food. I've got plenty of water, lemonade, and iced tea on ice in the coolers on the back of my truck."

"Day's a wasting. Let's get to it," Tommy called out.

"That's quite a surprise," Chad said, pulling Diana closer, wanting to show his appreciation with a well-deserved kiss...on the cheek. Too many people standing around, including Lindsey, to let her know just how much he appreciated her efforts.

He was still unable to believe what was happening. There must be over thirty-five guys there, all ready to chip in. All people from Crossroads Creek. There was no way he could ever assume the town hated him after this. Apparently, he had a lot to learn. And with Diana by his side, he was looking forward to the education.

"I knew," Lindsey said, happy to be in on the surprise.

"We all did. Diana put it together and the rest of us worked out the details. Your sister included," John said, setting the record straight.

"Well, I'll be." He turned to look at the group, watching as they started to set up workgroups. Jerry ran a construction company and took charge of the men, calling out orders. "Looks like it's time to get to work. I can't thank you all enough."

He turned to Diana, not having let go of her hand. "And as for you," he dropped a kiss on her lips, not caring who saw them, "a special thank you. You can be a mighty force to reckon with when you want something. This is quite a blessing."

Diana blushed, her cheeks turning a bright shade of pink. "You're welcome. Anything for my favorite cowboy."

"I've got to get to work, but later, there's something I want to talk to you about." Chad wouldn't let Diana go another night without knowing just how deeply he loved her.

"Sure thing. Hopefully, it's a good discussion," she said, the curiosity in her voice coming across loud and clear.

"You could say that." Chad dropped a kiss on Lindsey's forehead. "Thanks, Munchkin."

Hours passed, the teams working together to make it happen. Stud by stud, wall board by wall board. As a town team pulling together, the miracle of miracles happened. The barn was framed, enclosed with exterior walls and the roof put on. *All in one day.*

Everything was cleaned up, farewells and heartfelt gratitude flowing freely for all the guys had done. And to the women who'd shown up with food. It had been like a community BBQ, with so much to eat it would take weeks to finish what was left over.

Chad stepped back to check out the handiwork, feeling unbelievably blessed. Crossroads

Creek townsfolk had shown him he belonged. No more running, emotionally or physically. He was here to stay, and hopefully, with Diana by his side.

Something he'd know all too soon. As if in thinking of her, she appeared by his side.

"Lindsey's with your sister in the house. She's been wound up all day and I've got her trying to calm down so she'll sleep tonight when we get back to the inn." Diana laughed.

Chad nodded. "Sounds like a good plan. I did notice her out chasing the chickens at one point, which can be an unrewarding and ex-hausting game."

"True. *Ummm*, you said you wanted to talk to me, so let's talk. I've been curious all day," Di-ana said, pushing the conversation to the front and center of attention between them.

"I did at that." Chad took her by the hand and led her around the barn. The sun was just beginning to dip down past the horizon.

"It's beautiful," Diana said, gazing off into the distance.

"She sure is," Chad said, but he was looking at the love of his life, not the sunset.

Diana turned her gaze to his, a shy smile on her face.

Chad pulled the black velvet bag from his shirt pocket. He had bought the ring in town and had kept it close to his heart all day today as he worked, waiting for the right moment. Dropping to one knee, Diana's smile was the assurance her answer would be all that he'd hoped for. "I love you with all of my heart and all of my soul. You're the other half of me that I needed to find and the part that makes all this..." he waved his arm around to indicate the farm, "right. You and Lindsey bring such joy and peace to my life, and if you'll have me, I'd like to make you my wife. Diana Langley, will you marry me?"

Tears trickled down her face as she threw herself into his arms, Chad standing to keep from toppling over. "Yes. Yes. Yes, I'll marry you. I love you so much. And Lindsey loves you. You've been such a good role model for her and I couldn't think of a better man to be a father to my daughter."

Chad grinned. A dream was coming true in a way he'd never expected when he first met Diana. *Love in the country with a beautiful family to call his own.* He hugged her tight, saying a silent prayer of thanks.

"Oh wait, there is one condition," Diana exclaimed, pulling back slightly.

Chad wasn't overly worried, considering the love shining in her eyes. "What's that?"

"Marry me Sunday."

Chad chuckled. It was a simple request. "Which Sunday? There are fifty-two every year."

"This Sunday. Tomorrow. Right here in the barn *after we* go to church. No frills. Just a sunset wedding," Diana said, laying out her conditions.

The words *after we* came out loud and strong, but Chad didn't mind. He'd go anywhere with his beautiful fiancé. "Every woman dreams of her wedding day and plans to make the most memorable day of her life. Why would we do this tomorrow and ruin all that for you?"

"We have plenty of food already, and we can keep everything simple, but fun. All we need is music and Pastor Phil, and we can invite everyone."

"Well, okay then, if you're sure. But what about a fancy dress? Do you have something already? You can't get married without a special dress," Chad insisted, not wanting anything to ruin the special day when they declared their love for one another before God and the people in town.

"I don't need a fancy dress if I have you," Diana insisted.

"I knew I was marrying the right woman." Chad picked her up in his arms and twirled her around. "Yes, my soon to be darling wife, I'll marry you tomorrow."

Epilogue

TEN MONTHS LATER...

Diana gently rubbed her belly to calm baby Joshua, who was anxious to make his appearance into the world. Her parents were due to arrive this afternoon, as they were coming to stay a few weeks to help with Lindsey and the new baby. Having missed the wedding, they were thrilled with the invitation to stay at the farm and spend time together.

Her wedding day had gone off without a hitch. Chad had gone above and beyond to shower her with love and a huge surprise. He considered it a lovely payback for her surprise when the town had helped rebuild the barn. Diana smiled, touching their wedding photo on the mantel.

Chad's out of town milk business had led to several connections, one of which turned out to be a dress shop. A special delivery arrived before the wedding, and not of the milk kind. A gorgeous wedding gown, a sweet flower girl dress for Lindsey, and a lovely bridesmaid dress for Roxanne.

Beautiful gowns for the beautiful women in his life. That's how Chad described his generosity.

Love had been the theme of the day and no fancy setting could ever replace the barn where she'd said *I do.* With fairy tale twinkling lights and country music where guests danced under the stars, the entire impromptu event couldn't have been more perfect.

"They're here, Mommy," Lindsey called out excitedly from the window. She ran toward the door.

Diana, on the other hand, waddled. "I'm coming. Your brother is slowing me down these days," she said, laughing. It was the first time she'd seen her parents in a little over a year, and she couldn't help but be happy. A year was a long time...long enough for them to have some heart-to-heart video chats. And long enough to repair their relationship.

Chad, bless his heart, made it so she had plenty of time to get ready for the baby. He'd hired some full-time help on the farm, insisting she take it easy. The farm was flourishing, and although he'd been against her putting cash into the place at first, she'd finally convinced him they were a partnership in every sense of the word. The decision to move into a bigger dairy farming arena had been made easier when one of their neighbors decided to sell their ranch. From three hundred acres to seven hundred and fifty, they were mainstream and profitable, their cows producing some of the best hormone and antibiotic free organic milk. With close to five hundred head of cows, and a second, larger barn with automated milking free stalls, they had increased their orders and their profitability exponentially.

And even with all that going on, they'd fixed up Chad's childhood fort, turning it into their own special place for romantic getaways overlooking the river. And most likely the place where Joshua was conceived not long after the wedding.

Lindsey would get a new fort of her own, but one much closer to the house. "Grandma," Lindsey called out as she ran out the door to greet them.

"How's my darling granddaughter?" her mother asked, giving Lindsey a big hug as Diana's father joined the group.

"I'm your *only* granddaughter, silly. But I'm good. Look," she said, pointing to Diana's belly. "Mommy is as big as a house cause that's my brother in there." Lindsey was more than a little excited about her brother, although her patience was wearing thin. Nine months was a long time to wait.

"Big baby," her mother commented, grinning up at Diana.

"Hi, Mom. It's so good to see you. And you can say that again. For a while we started to wonder about twins." Diana grimaced, unsure how anyone handles multiple births at once. She had all she could do to get ready for the arrival of one.

"This is such an exciting time for us all. New beginnings and a new baby." Her mother leaned in for a hug, sandwiching the baby in between them. Her father followed suit. "Hey, Dad. I'm glad you could make it."

"Wouldn't miss it for the world. Selling out the business to the Gibson's was the right decision. With Silas in prison, it made things tense for everyone involved."

It wasn't a subject anyone brought up often, but at least it would lay the past to rest. "What do you plan to do now?" Diana asked. It was a lot to take in and the worry she'd irrevocably damaged what her parents had once believed was their nest egg was a lot of responsibility. Not that they laid any blame at her feet.

Her father grinned, an all-knowing look passing between Diana's parents. "Oh, we thought we would check out some property near here. After all, this is where our daughter, son-in-law, and two grandchildren are, so what better place for us in order to be closer?"

Diana's mouth dropped open to form a wide "O." It took a few seconds to recover. "That would be wonderful. I can't believe you would leave the city."

"Well, there are a lot of things I can't believe either, but we learned life is for living and love, and it was time for us to slow things down and enjoy ourselves," her mother said, joining in the discussion.

Chad suddenly appeared on the porch, her handsome husband always making her smile.

"I thought I saw you all pull up to the house. It's nice to meet you in person," Chad said, extending his hand in greeting.

"None of that, young man. We're family," his mother said, giving Chad a hug like they were old friends.

Proof that people can change for the better.

Her father and Chad shook hands. "Thanks for taking such good care of my daughter and granddaughter. Diana sure knows how to pick them...way better than we did," he said, shaking his head as if remembering the past with distaste.

"My pleasure, David. I promise you, taking care of them brings me far greater joy than you could imagine."

"Great to know," her father said.

"Forgive and forget. That's our motto, Dad," Diana added. They would need to forgive themselves if they wanted to embrace happiness. It was the same message the people in Crossroads Creek had recently figured out, much to the satisfaction of everyone concerned.

Her dad nodded. "I do like the sound of that."

"I need to get inside out of this heat if you all don't mind. It's not quite like New York weather," her mother said, smiling at Diana. "And I'm sure you need to get off your feet."

"I do." It was quite hot, and she did feel a little out of sorts. Air conditioning and a chair sounded heavenly.

"Can I take Grandpa down to see my horse?" Lindsey asked.

"Sure thing, Munchkin," Chad said, stepping back to let them pass. "I'll go inside with your mother and make sure she has everything she needs and show your grandmother around. Just remember the rules, Lindsey, and don't open any stall gates. Oh, and be sure to let Allison know I'll be down to help her with the milking shortly."

"Yes, sir," Lindsey called out as she skipped off, her grandfather barely managing to keep up.

Allison had left New York without so much as moment's hesitation when Diana had offered the job as quality control manager over the new herd and the expansion process. Who better to handle the job than someone who had been successfully managing people for as long as Diana could remember? Someone they loved and trusted and had been a blessing to all.

Chad settled his hand around Diana's waist to help her inside the house. Her protective husband never missed an opportunity to be close. *Cherished.* The perfect word to describe the way he made her feel. They headed for the kitchen, Chad pouring her a glass of iced tea.

"I'll be right back to show you around the house, Virginia," Chad said, moving off down the hall.

Diana sat down at the table, the overwhelming relief to be off her feet a Godsend. She sipped at the iced tea, watching as little rivulets danced down the sides of the glass as the cold met the warmer room temperatures. A pool of water formed at the base, and she used a napkin to soak it up. Reaching for the glass, she leaned forward to take another sip. The glass slid out of her hand, landing hard on the table as a rocketing pain caught her off guard.

"Are you okay, dear?' her mother exclaimed, rushing to her side.

"Yes. I think so, anyway. I'm almost positive it's just another Braxton Hicks contraction. I've been having them a lot lately, but I've got another week until the baby—" Diana grabbed her abdomen, another cramp hitting, stronger this time.

Her mother brushed her hair aside, staying nearby and eyeing her doubtfully. "I don't know, honey. Maybe we should have you checked out."

"Let's give it more time. See what happens." Twice she'd already been to the hospital, and each time they sent her home. *Too soon.*

Three minutes later, there was no doubt in Diana's mind what was happening. Braxton Hicks were a thing of the past. "I think you're right, Mom. It's time. *Ummm*, Chad," she called out.

Chad rushed into the kitchen, as if sensing the urgency in her voice. "Yes, what's wrong?" he asked after taking one look at her.

The anticipation of what was to come had sent her heart racing, but Chad's presence was calming. Exactly what she needed as she tried to breathe through the next contraction. "Baby Joshua is trying to make his arrival early."

"Again? Do you think it's for real this time?" he asked, his eyes growing wide.

He was such a good sport the other two times. "Yes. Seeing as my water just broke, I'd say this is not a trial run." A simple case of third times the charm.

"What do we do?" he asked, suddenly more flustered than she'd ever seen him, including the first two times.

Diana smiled. The realness of it all had turned him into a panicky father-to-be, and it was up to her to get things under control. At least for now. "Calm down and breathe, for starters. Go get the bag we prepared and pull the truck up closer to the front porch." Diana tried to laugh, but a contraction hit. "Mom, can you go alert the others? Allison will know what to do with Lindsey and Chad will drive me to the medical center."

"Gotcha. How exciting," her mother said, her eyes lit with wonder.

"Tell that to Chad," Diana quipped, clutching her belly. She knew the routine. Delivery was no picnic, but then there would be great joy as she held her baby in her arms for the first time.

They arrived at the medical center and Chad finally settled his nerves as he looked around, seeing another expectant father waiting in the wings and pacing the hall. He wanted to be strong for Diana, and her husband managed it like a pro.

Two hours later, Joshua let out a cry that brought tears to her eyes as she took her son from the doctor. *A tiny piece of Godly perfection.*

And the moment Diana handed the baby to Chad, the expression on his face was one of reverence. *And totally priceless.*

"He's amazing," Chad said, his voice a mere whisper. Clearly, he had fallen in love instantly.

"Just like his daddy," Diana said, reaching out to touch her husband's arm. "I love you."

"I love you, too," Chad said, leaning over to drop a kiss on her forehead. "And I love you—son."

He kissed Joshua's forehead gently, his gaze never leaving the baby.

It would seem that although her cowboy started out helping her, in the end, they had helped each other. *To true love and happiness.*

What to Read Next...

The Return of a Cowboy
If you enjoyed this sweet and charming romance, be sure to check out the
ALSO BY ELSIE DAVIS section on the next page for more clean and wholesome romance.

BONUS READ

Want to keep in touch with new releases and what's happening in the world of Elsie Davis?

Sign up for the monthly newsletter at (https://www.elsiedavishea.com) Elsie Davis HEA (Happily-Ever-After) and enjoy DIGGING THE DRIVER (A Celebrity Corgi Romance) as a FREE BOOK!

The greatest compliment you could give an author is to leave a review in order to help other readers discover the same great stories you enjoyed. Amazon/Bookbub/Goodreads are all great places. Many thanks!!!

Another great way to keep in touch - *Follow Elsie Davis on FaceBook*

Also By Elsie Davis

Sweet, Clean and Wholesome Stories...with a Happily-Ever-After Guarantee!

Holidays in Hallbrook

(Sweet Romance Series for Holidays Throughout the Year)

Welcome to Hallbrook, New Hampshire. A small-town filled with the unexpected, lots of love, and of course, a beloved dog to ramp up the excitement.

Love & Order (Labor Day)

Love & Family (Thanksgiving)

Love & Peace (Christmas)

Love & Chocolate (Valentine's Day)

Love & Hope (Mother's Day)

Love & Liberty (Independence Day)

Love & Honor (Veteran's Day)

Love & Joy (Easter)

Love & Adventure (Father's Day)

Great Smoky Mountain Getaways

(Christian Inspirational – Women's Fiction Romances)

Juliet's Journey to Love

Poppy's Path to Love

Rachel's Road to Love

Crossroads Creek Cowboys

(Christian Inspirational Romances)

The Heart of a Cowboy

The Help of a Cowboy

The Return of a Cowboy

Coming Soon – The Care of a Cowboy

Crestfield Inn Romances

If you like special kinds of soulmates, a splash of the supernatural, and wholesome relationships, you'll adore this sweet bit of fun filled with romance and mystery.

Turning Back Time

Turning Up Roses

Turning Down Pie

Celebrity Corgi Romance

(Standalone Sweet Romance)

If you like light mystery mixed in with your happily-ever-after, you'll enjoy this second-chance romance and the race to save an adorable Corgi.

Digging the Driver

Gold Coast Retrievers

(Sweet Romance)

Special Golden Retrievers help their humans solve mysteries, save lives, and even find love...

Defending Dakota

Trinity River

(Sweet Western Romance)

Ranchers and farmers depend on the Trinity River for water, but when a secret conglomerate starts buying up property by fair means or foul, it's time for the landowners of Tumble County to fight back—Texas style. But what they don't count on, is finding love in the process.

Back in the Rancher's Arms

Small Town, Big Secrets

Coming Soon! (2023-2024)

Sundancer's Legacy – 9 Book series

Sundancer's Star

Sundancer's Joy

Sundancer's Heart

Sundancer's Majesty

Sundancer's Miracle

Sundancer's Glory

Sundancer's Kiss

Sundancer's Moon

Sundancer's Splendor

About The Author

Elsie Davis is a *USA Today and International Bestselling Author* of over 25 sweet, clean, and wholesome romances, and a member of the ACFW. She discovered the world of Happily-Ever-After romance at the age of twelve when she began avidly reading Barbara Cartland, the Queen of Romance, and has been hooked ever since. After building her dream log home on top of a small mountain, she turned her attention to do what she loves most, writing. Elsie writes sweet Contemporary Romance and Contemporary Christian Romance from her heart...hoping to share a little love in a big world.

When she's not writing, she can be found birding, kayaking, camping, fishing, playing disc golf, and taking nature walks—hoping to spot wildlife. Basically, she loves all things outdoors, EXCEPT cold weather. She and her husband are avid Caribbean cruisers, but Elsie's favorite vacation was their cruise to Alaska. (In spite of the cold!) Indoors, she enjoys a toasty fire, and of course, a great romance with a guaranteed Happily-Ever-After.

https://www.elsiedavishea.com

www.ingramcontent.com/pod-product-compliance
Lightning Source LLC
Chambersburg PA
CBHW051318190726
48290CB00001B/209